BY Matt

KILLER Vending Machines WRECKED My Lunch!

ILLUSTRATED BY PACO SORDO

USBORNE

FRIDAY

ALONE

Drishya Samode opened her curtains and let out a bone-chilling scream.

"AAAGGGGHHHHHHHHHHHHHH!"

A face was staring back at her from the window. A hideous, ghostly face with bloodshot eyes and wild, sticky-up hair.

"AAAGGGGHHHHHHHHHHHHHH!"

Drishya screamed again until she realized that the face wasn't an angry ghost, or a twenty-foot

tall giant who wanted to snatch her from her bedroom and kidnap her. The sun hadn't quite risen and it was still dark enough outside for her window to reflect her own face back at her. The hideous, terrifying face of a recently-woken eleven year old.

Drishya stared at her reflection and was ruffling her dark, tangled hair, when a flash of light coming from the street below distracted her. She looked down as a huge lorry turned into her cul-de-sac and parked outside the house opposite. It was a house that Drishya knew every inch of. A house that Drishya had spent almost as much time in as her own. It was the house that had, until recently, belonged to Drishya's best friend, Hattie Lavernock.

Hattie and her family had moved out barely a fortnight ago but Drishya missed her so much it already felt like a lifetime. Hattie's parents had decided that after recent "events" they would move out of Dreary Inkling and start a new life somewhere else.

"It's just not safe here," Hattie's mum had said when Drishya had asked why they were moving. "Who knows what's going to happen next? This whole town is cursed. CURSED, I TELL YOU!"

Honestly, it was such an overreaction to a couple of tiny incidents of potential global devastation. First, there had been that time a couple of months ago when two aliens had very nearly blown up the whole planet after watching a talent show at Drishya's school*. And then there was the school trip a few weeks ago when an evil witch had tried to become supreme ruler of the world by turning Drishya's entire class into an army of brain-sucking zombies**.

"But there's no way anything like that could ever happen again here," Drishya had said to Mrs Lavernock, trying to reason with her. "The odds of worldwide destruction happening in Dreary Inkling for a *third* time must be a hundred billion billion billion to one!"

But it was no use and Hattie had gone, and

---

* The whole unbelievably exciting and fabulously well-written story can be found in the brilliant book, *Aliens Invaded My Talent Show!*
** For the lowdown on that extraordinary tale, just get yourself a copy of *Mutant Zombies Cursed My School Trip!* Believe me, it'll blow your flippin' socks off, unless you're not wearing any socks, in which case, it'll blow your feet off. So, it's probably best to make sure you're wearing socks.

now a new family were moving in to Kinney Avenue. Drishya felt a knot in her stomach at the thought of another whole day of school without her best friend. As she closed her curtains, she heard an enormous bang coming from downstairs. This was followed by the sound of her dad yelling, and then what sounded like the sound of her dad sobbing. Drishya grabbed her dressing gown and ran downstairs.

"Everything okay, Dad?" she said, racing into the kitchen.

Mr Samode was holding a bin bag in his hands and had a crazed, panicky look etched on his face. The same crazed, panicky look he'd had on his face when he'd accidentally called Drishya's teacher "Mummy" at her last parents' evening.

"BIN JUICE!" he yelled. "THE BIN JUICE IS DRIPPING ON ME."

Drishya saw that liquid from the bottom of the bin bag was dripping on his slippers. He screwed his face up and held the bag at arm's length.

"It's so stinky," he said, gagging. "And slimy. And horrible."

Then he ran to the back door, opened it and charged out into the garden in the direction of the recycling bins. After a couple of minutes, he reappeared panting heavily. Drishya rolled

her eyes. Her dad was
never at his best in
the morning.

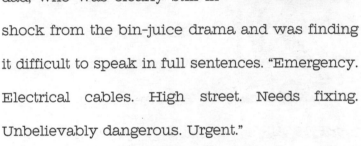

"Where's Mum?"
asked Drishya.

"Early callout," said her
dad, who was clearly still in
shock from the bin-juice drama and was finding
it difficult to speak in full sentences. "Emergency.
Electrical cables. High street. Needs fixing.
Unbelievably dangerous. Urgent."

Drishya's mum worked as an engineer for the
local electricity company. She'd only recently got
the job and this was the first time she'd been on
an emergency callout, which meant that this was
the first time Drishya's dad had been on his own

during the Samode early morning routine.

"I miss her so very, very much," he said, blowing his nose into a tea towel.

Drishya sighed.

"It's okay, Dad," she said. "I'm sure we'll get through it. I tell you what, why don't I get myself some breakfast while you go and put some trousers on?"

Drishya's dad looked at her for a moment and then down at his bare legs.

"TROUSERS!" he yelled, running out of the kitchen and up the stairs. "I COMPLETELY FORGOT MY TROUSERS!"

Drishya could tell that it was going to be a long morning.

THE ROBOCALYPSE IS COMING

Drishya sat down in her favourite chair and pushed a button on the remote control. The TV flickered into life and the doughy face of local news presenter, Jonathan Bonathan-Jovington, appeared.

"Good morning, Dreary Inkling," he said, in a very important-sounding voice.

Drishya eagerly shovelled a spoonful of cornflakes into her mouth. The local morning news show was usually duller than an unbuttered crumpet but Drishya wondered if they might talk about the emergency that her mum had gone to sort out.

"The big story this morning," he said, with a look on his face like his underpants were a bit too tight, "is the news that Dreary Inkling billionaire and celebrity, Noel Skum, is unveiling a brand-new product." He paused dramatically. "So, we can now go LIVE to Skum Industries HQ."

The television picture cut from the studio to a picture of a very large building. And right next to the building was a pair of enormous speakers.

Drishya grabbed the remote control and turned up the volume; she didn't want to miss a second of this. She absolutely loved Noel Skum. He was head of Skum Industries 2000, one of the most innovative companies in the world. They had done all kinds of amazing things like designing super-fast microchips, creating a range of bestselling soft drinks, and developing a smart-suit for really important people who were so busy they didn't even have time to go to the toilet. The smart-clothes allowed the wearer to go to the toilet inside the suit itself, meaning that a top executive could be in a long meeting and not have to leave the room if they needed a wee. Suddenly, a huge fanfare blasted out of the speakers and Drishya spotted something happening right at the top of the building. The camera zoomed in on a mysterious figure wearing a jet-pack, who jumped off the roof and flew down to the ground. The mysterious figure had on a silver helmet and sunglasses but Drishya knew exactly who it was because they were dressed in an all-in-one black jumpsuit with matching cape attachment and white cowboy boots. The same all-in-one black jumpsuit with matching cape attachment and white cowboy boots that they always wore. The mysterious figure landed perfectly, right in front of the building, and took off his helmet.

"Hi, I'm Noel Skum!"

Another fanfare blared out of the speakers. Noel Skum smiled an enormous smile.

"I'm delighted to be here this morning, outside my enormous building, that I own, to share something BRAND-NEW that I invented, all by myself."

Noel Skum held up a green packet.

"Get ready for..."

The camera zoomed right into the green packet that Noel Skum was holding. Drishya stared at the TV with a ferocious intensity. She could see the word SKUMSNAX on the side of the packet in fancy gold writing.

"Sku-umSnax," blared a choir from out of the speakers.

"Sku-umSnax," sang Drishya, who was completely wrapped up in the moment.

"That's right," said Noel Skum, opening up the packet and picking out one of the snacks. "SkumSnax. A new range of the most highly-delicious snacks the world has ever seen in three INCREDIBLE flavours, that I came up with: cheese and pickled egg, banana and prawn, and chocolatey beef."

With a large explosion, cannons fired sparkling silver confetti into the air as Noel Skum put his helmet back on and fired up his jet-pack.

"They're available to buy right now, across the country, from special vending machines that I also invented, and will completely change the way you snack."

And with that, Noel Skum pushed the button on his jet-pack.

"SkumSnax. Where flavour is concerned, the sky's the limit!" he shouted as he launched himself back into the air and flew away.

The picture cut back to the studio where Jonathan Bonathan-Jovington was standing up, behind his desk, and applauding.

"INCREDIBLE!" he shouted, shaking his head in disbelief. "There's always excitement when Noel Skum's around."

Drishya blew out her cheeks and was marvelling at how AMAZING SkumSnax sounded, when she heard her dad yelling her name.

"DRISHYA! YOU NEED TO GET READY OR WE'LL BE LATE!"

Drishya shovelled the rest of her cereal into her mouth and was just about to turn off the TV when the news cut away to an advert. Suddenly, the screen was full of small robot machines smashing up other small robot machines.

"CALLING ALL FANS OF *ROBOCALYPSE*!" screamed the advert.

"THE HIT TV SHOW IS COMING TO FILM IN DREARY INKLING NEXT FRIDAY NIGHT."

Drishya's jaw stopped mid-chew and mushed-up cereal and milk began falling out of her open mouth. **ROBOCALYPSE** was Drishya's absolute favourite TV show in the whole of the actual world. **ROBOCALYPSE** was a robot warrior gameshow, where people built robots that would fight against each other to the cyber-death. Drishya had been so inspired by the show that she had even started trying to build her own robots. In fact, ever since she had seen her first **ROBOCALYPSE** episode, Drishya had dreamed that one day, she would be part of a **ROBOCALYPSE** team, walking down the Corridor of Carnage, through the Doorway of Devastation and stepping out into the Arena of Annihilation.

"THE SHOW NEEDS YOU," yelled the advert as a robot exploded into flames. "IF YOU'VE GOT A ROBOT AND A TEAM, COME DOWN TO THE SPECIALLY-BUILT ARENA IN DREARY INKLING PARK ON FRIDAY AT SIX P.M."

Drishya couldn't believe it – this was her chance. She knew right there and right then that she had to enter **ROBOCALYPSE**. All she needed to do was form a team to take part and build an insane fighting robot in the next seven days.

There must be loads of kids who love **ROBOCALYPSE**, she thought, then chuckled to herself. *And if there aren't then I could just set up a team with Noel Skum, which would be UN-BE-*

FLIPPIN'-LIEVABLE. Imagine the kind of robots he could build.

And for the first time in nearly two weeks, Drishya wasn't thinking about how much she missed Hattie as she got ready for school. She was daydreaming about controlling robots that killed other robots and lifting the **ROBOCALYPSE** trophy.

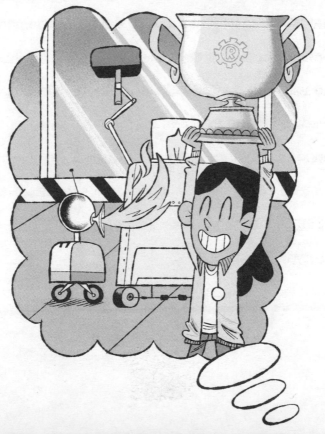

G.E.O.F.F.

That morning, Drishya hadn't paid a single scrap of attention to any of her lessons.

She could have just sat through a lesson of Swedish Mountain Wrestling followed by a double period of Advanced Troll Hunting for all she had taken in. And, as she stood at the back of the lunch queue, there was still only one thing on Drishya's mind:

Well, **ROBOCALYPSE** and the rather unpleasan
smell of broccoli that filled the lunch hall. But the
rather unpleasant smell of broccoli filled the lunch
hall almost every day, so that was nothing new.
Throughout the morning, Drishya had been trying
to recruit someone to be part of her robotic
building team. She had sent out a whole load of
secret notes during morning lessons but, so far,
everyone had turned her down.

Drishya tucked her hair behind her ear, pulled
a notebook out of her rucksack and began flicking
through it. A notebook she hadn't even looked at
for months, mainly because Hattie hadn't liked
robots and so they had done other things together.
But after seeing the **ROBOCALYPSE** advert that
morning, Drishya had grabbed the notebook

before she left for school. It was full of pages and pages of drawings and designs and doodles for the ultimate battle bot.

It had all started two years ago when Drishya had been off school for a week with chickenpox. She'd spent most of the week lying on the sofa watching TV. One day, while she was flicking through the hundreds of channels, Drishya saw something that immediately caught her attention. It was the sight of a small robot bashing another, larger robot to smithereens with a huge hammer that was coming out of its back. Drishya didn't know it at the time but she had just witnessed Smash Gordon's epic takedown of the Choppersaurus. The channel she was watching was in the middle of a twenty-four-hour, nonstop **ROBOCALYPSE** marathon and Drishya was hooked. For the rest of the day she sat open-mouthed and goggle-eyed as Smash Gordon defeated Tyrannosaurus Wreckage, then Gladys Fight, then Saw Tooth, then Brian Damage, then Sir Crush-a-lot, then Little Miss Carnage, then the Power and the Gory. By the time Drishya went back to school, she had started to draw her own battle bots.

She glanced at the first page of the notebook and looked at the first bot she had thought up: the Demon Destroyer. She smiled at the memory of how much time she had spent on it, trying to make sure that everything was perfect. It was obvious to her now expert eye that it would never have worked properly. But working on the

Demon Destroyer had inspired Drishya to come up with her next battle bot, Driller Killer. It was better than the Demon Destroyer but still not quite right.

"The drill bit is way too thin, it'd snap off like a twig," Drishya muttered to herself, turning the page.

After Driller Killer came the Ultimate Typhoon. This was the first of her battle bots that Drishya had ever tried to build. It was not a success. Drishya had tried to use an old silver tea tray that she'd found at the back of a cupboard as armour-plating by hammering it into shape. But then her mum had seen what she was doing and had gone berserk because apparently the tea tray was a family heirloom that had been handed down from mother to daughter in her family for generations. Drishya tried to point out to her mum that it would eventually have

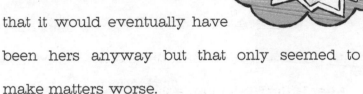

been hers anyway but that only seemed to make matters worse.

Drishya flicked through some more pages until she came to her best battle bot. The biggest, the baddest, the most intense battle bot warrior she had ever imagined. The Gigantic Extreme Orange Fighting Fiend, aka G.E.O.F.F.

G.E.O.F.F. was big and powerful. Its body was

a shallow dome shape, covered with bright orange battle armour, and from out of its back curled a large, thick tail that tapered to a sharp point. This tail was capable of stabbing through almost anything that it came across. G.E.O.F.F. looked a bit like a huge turtle, albeit a completely awesome turtle who would probably kill you if you got in its way. She stared at G.E.O.F.F. and thought how perfect it would be for **ROBOCALYPSE**.

"CHOICE!"

Drishya looked up from her notebook and realized that she was suddenly at the front of the lunch queue.

"CHOICE?" bellowed the terrifying Mrs Clutch, holding a ladle in her hand like she was about to attack a charging rhino.

Drishya marvelled at the extraordinary combination of purple lipstick and green eyeshadow that looked like it had been trowelled onto Mrs Clutch's face by a particularly spiteful chimpanzee. Beads of sweat gathered on her wrinkled brow and Drishya stood, hypnotized, as one droplet of perspiration trickled down her bulbous veiny nose. The sweat stopped and quivered for the briefest of moments, before falling with a plop into the waiting jug of custard below.

"CHOICE?" yelled Mrs Clutch, again.

Drishya looked at the trays of food in front of her and surveyed her two main-course options:

1. Something that was labelled "chicken stew and rice" but actually looked like a plateful of cat sick.

2. Something that claimed to be the "vegetarian option" but really looked like enormous lumps of earwax, sprinkled with dried earwax, and covered in a greeny browny sludge that was the colour of earwax.

"Er, what's that?" said Drishya.

Mrs Clutch picked her nose. "Veggie ravioli," she said. "You wannit?"

Drishya had been a vegetarian her entire life and so didn't have much choice. She nodded sadly and Mrs Clutch dipped her ladle into the greeny brown gloop and slopped some onto a plate. She handed it to Drishya and gave her one last withering look before turning to serve Ian Iansson, who was standing just behind her.

"CHOICE!" she bawled.

Drishya sighed and gloomily took her tray. She didn't realize it but as she looked for somewhere to sit, Drishya was being watched. In fact, not just one, but three people had been secretly watching her all morning.

THE DREAM SQUAD

"Now then," said Drishya under her breath, scanning the hall for signs of engineering expertise. "Who looks like they might want to be part of an elite team of robot builders?"

She saw Max Frameraté and Jonny Smuthers from Year Four throwing peas at the wall to see if they would stick.

"Not them," muttered Drishya, mentally ticking them off her list of people to ask to be in her

ROBOCALYPSE team.

Then she saw Judith Priest and Dan Halen from Year Five slopping chicken stew and mashed potato onto their table and using it to make weird-looking sculptures.

"Not them, either," she said to herself with a sigh. "This is hopeless. I need to find some people who I want to hang out with, and who want to be part of a team with me. But at this rate, finding anyone will take ages."

Just then she heard a voice from behind her.

"Hi, Drishya!"

Drishya spun around and saw Janet Krapplehoff smiling at her, her long, perfectly-brushed hair shimmering under the canteen lights. Janet nodded over to a table on the other side of the hall where Drishya saw Brianna Grimditch and Kimberley Armitage smiling and waving at her.

"Wanna come and sit with us?" said Janet, putting an arm around Drishya's shoulder.

Drishya gulped. Brianna, Janet and Kimberley were no ordinary Year Six girls. They were the

Dream Squad, the three coolest girls in the whole school. They were so cool that they all wore berets, all the time, even in lessons. They were admired and feared with equal measure because even though they always looked amazing, they could be mean too. Really mean.

Brianna Grimditch

Age: 10

Likes: Wearing berets and gymnastics

Dislikes: Uncool people aka anyone not in the Dream Squad

Special Moves: Bold hands-on-hips and hands-off-hips

Janet Krapplehoff

Age: 11 (in two weeks and three days)

Likes: Berets and the word "like"

Dislikes: All hats other than berets

Special Moves: Super-fast hair flicks and intense staring

Kimberley Armitage

Age: 10

Likes: Berets and football

Dislikes: Flutes (too tooty), ballet costumes (too tu-tu) and the second number of the eleven times table (too two-two)

Special Moves: "Scissor Kicks" and ability to wear a beret in an extremely cool way

"Er, er, okay," said Drishya.

"Ve-some," said Janet, which meant **very awesome**. The Dream Squad loved shoving words together to make new words. "Come and chalax (**cha**t + re**lax**) with us. We have something that we simply *have* to ask you about."

As Drishya followed Janet to the Dream Squad's table, she thought about whether she should ask them to be in her ROBOCALYPSE team. They wouldn't have been her first choice but, then again, time was running out and if she didn't have a team, she wouldn't be able to compete. Drishya set her tray down on the table and smiled nervously at the coolest girls in the whole school. The Dream Squad might just be her last hope.

THE LEGENDARY CARDIGAN OF PEACHY KEENE

Drishya realized immediately that there was something strange going on. Janet and Kimberley were whispering to each other and giggling when they looked at her. Then, when Drishya sat down, Brianna leaned over and started stroking Drishya's hair.

"Hey there, Drishya," said Brianna in a sing-song voice. "It's so ve-some that you're sitting with us."

Drishya rubbed the back of her neck.

"Er, yeah, right, great," she said, nervously.

Kimberley let out an uncontrollable shrieking laugh. Brianna snapped her head around and stared at Kimberley. Kimberley covered her mouth and stopped laughing. Now that she was sitting with them, Drishya wasn't at all sure about asking them to be in her **ROBOCALYPSE** team.

"So, like, we were, like, just chatting," said Janet, who always seemed to end every sentence by going up at the end, like it was a question, "when we, like, totally eyeballed you wearing that teemazing (totally + **amazing**) cardigan."

Drishya looked down at her cardie. It seemed pretty ordinary to her. Her mum had got it at the school's second-hand uniform sale the day before.

"We just wondered if you'd mind us having a closer look at it?" said Brianna, holding out her hand.

Drishya looked at the Dream Squad. All of them were watching her, eyes wide, waiting for a response. Drishya nodded and began unbuttoning her cardigan.

"Er, okay," she said, giving it to Brianna. "Look, this may be a stupid question but do any of you guys like watching the TV show *Robocalyp*—"

Brianna held up a hand to silence Drishya as she stared at her cardie. Janet started breathing really weirdly as Brianna gently ran her fingers over the fabric, like she was examining an ancient text.

"Is it real?" whispered Kimberley.

Brianna turned the sleeve over and pointed a quivering finger at a hole on the left cuff.

"Look!" she said. "It's the hole."

Brianna looked inside, searching every inch of the cardigan until she found what she was looking for. The Dream Squad gasped. Brianna held the cardigan by the washing instructions label. There, for all of them to see, written in black indelible pen, were the initials PK.

"It is real," said Kimberley, her voice hushed.

"It's really hers," whispered Janet.

"What?" asked Drishya. "Who are you talking about?"

Brianna looked at her.

"This," she said slowly, "is the cardigan of..." She lowered her voice to a whisper, "Peachy Keene."

Drishya looked at each of the girls.

"Oh, wow," she said, pausing for a moment before adding, "er, who's Peachy Keene?"

Brianna quickly scanned the hall to make sure no one was listening in to their conversation.

"Peachy Keene," she said slowly, "was the original member of the Dream Squad. Peachy and

Violet Crisps founded it eight years ago as a secret society that only the coolest girls in the school could join."

"Wow," said Drishya.

"Peachy Keene was, like, the most ve-some girl, like,

ever in the history of Dreary Inkling," said Janet.

"V ve-some," added Kimberley.

Brianna held up the sleeve of Drishya's cardigan. "This hole was the very first thumb hole ever created," she said. "Before Peachy Keene, no one had ever thought of making a hole in their sleeve for their thumb to go through. Her ideas on how to wear school uniform were years ahead of their time."

Brianna handed the cardigan back to Drishya. "And you have her cardigan," she said. "Which means that by the ancient eight-year-old laws of the Dream Squad, you could be the next member, if you want to be."

Drishya couldn't believe it. This was perfect. She needed some people to be part of her team and suddenly, for reasons she didn't fully understand, here were the three coolest girls in the school asking her to join the Dream Squad.

"Oh, that would be amazing," said Drishya, putting Peachy Keene's cardigan back on. It was weird but just doing up the buttons gave Drishya a kind of strange confidence that she hadn't ever had before. "So, do any of you ever watch ROBOCALYPSE?"

But the Dream Squad weren't listening to Drishya. They were huddled together whispering.

"Okay," said Brianna, after a few moments. "We can do the first initiation test right now."

The Dream Squad looked at each other and smiled wicked smiles.

"Initiation test?" said Drishya, her  voice cracking slightly with a note of nervousness.

"Of course," said Brianna. "You didn't think that we let just anyone join the Dream Squad, did you? If you want to be part of the team, you need to prove yourself."

Drishya gulped. She didn't like the sound of this but she needed to be part of a team.

"What's the first test?" she said.

"Well, all you have to do is give someone a fabulous new look," said Brianna. "Now, who shall we choose?"

She scanned the room for a few seconds and smiled as her eyes landed on Commodore Sinclair and Elton Gweek, two boys from their class, who were sitting a few tables away playing a game of chess on a small travel board.

"Ah," Brianna said, "they'll do perfectly."

Drishya stood by the Dream Squad's table, holding her plate loaded with disgusting-looking veggie ravioli.

"So let me get this straight," she said. "You want me to go over to Elton and throw this all over him?"

The Dream Squad nodded and giggled.

"That doesn't seem like a very nice thing to do," Drishya said. "Maybe I could do a different initiation?"

Brianna adjusted her beret and stared at Drishya. "The first rule of the Dream Squad," she said, "is that if you want to be a member then you have to do what we say."

"I thought that the first rule of the Dream Squad was about wearing berets," said Kimberley.

Brianna rolled her eyes. "No, that's the third rule of the Dream Squad," she said.

"So what's the second rule then?" said Janet.

"To always look like you couldn't care less about what anyone is saying," said Brianna, rolling her eyes and looking like she didn't care, at all.

As the Dream Squad worked out the specific order of the rules of the Dream Squad, Drishya looked over at Elton as he moved a rook across the chessboard. Even though they were in the same class, she hadn't really spoken much to him before. After making his move he smoothed down his immaculate side parting and tugged the cuff of his shirt so that it poked out of the sleeve of his jumper. Everything about Elton was always so neat and tidy and clean. Drishya watched him as he waited for Commodore to make his move. She noticed that Elton was turning something over in his hand. It was something small and grey with shiny gold legs. Drishya's heart skipped a beat.

"No way," she whispered. "That can't be."

Without really realizing it, Drishya started walking, like she was caught in the grip of a powerful spell.

Janet nudged Brianna. "She's going to do it, she's going to do it," she sniggered, as they watched Drishya move slowly across the hall until she reached Commodore and Elton's table.

Drishya stopped, still holding the tray.

"I-is that what I think it is?" she said, pointing at the thing Elton was holding.

Elton turned and looked at her. "Well," he said pushing up his glasses. "Were you thinking of a Skum Industries 2000 SKUM9 microchip? Because if you were, then yes it is."

Drishya stood staring at the processor, almost as if she were hypnotized by its beauty.

"That is SO awesome," she said.

Commodore blew a strand of his long shaggy hair out of his eyes.

"Uh huh," he agreed, in his low, slow drawl. "It is highly awesome."

Drishya looked at Commodore; his eyes were half shut and he was nodding his head gently and smiling. She noticed that he wore beads around his wrist, like a surfer.

"Where did you get it from?" she said, turning back to Elton.

"Er, this just in," said Elton, who had quite an annoying habit of saying "this just in" a lot, as if he was breaking important news like they did on the telly. "My dad only works in the factory that makes them."

"Wow," said Drishya, unable to contain her amazement. "Your dad works for Noel Skum?"

Elton nodded.

"Have you ever met him?" said Drishya.

Elton looked at Drishya. "My dad? Oh sure,

I see him all the time. Great guy," he said.

Drishya rolled her eyes. "No, Noel Skum, of course," she said.

Elton cleared his throat. "Well, sort of," he said, lowering his voice and looking around to make sure he couldn't be overheard. "He was supposed to come round to our house for a meeting with Dad. Dad got an email two days before with a list of weird things we had to do before Mr Skum turned up."

"Really," said Drishya. "Like what?"

"Well," said Elton. "Dad had to get a special seat ready for him, at least thirty centimetres taller than all the other chairs."

"That's a bit weird," said Drishya. "Why did he need that?"

"I don't know," said Elton. "Dad balanced a chair on top of some books and put six cushions on it for extra height. But that's not all."

Drishya moved a step closer.

"The email also said that we all had to wear white clothes," said Elton. "Because Mr Skum wanted us to contrast with his all-black outfit."

Drishya made a face. "That's a bit odd, too," she said.

"Yeah but that's not all," said Elton. "He also insisted that we make our living room look exactly like the living room in his house. He sent us photos and everything."

"Weird," said Drishya.

Elton nodded. "I know, especially because he has a life-size statue of himself in his living room," he said. "It took us ages to make one with egg boxes and tinfoil."

"Woah," smiled Commodore, his eyes still half-closed. "Sounds totally rad."

"So, what was he like?" said Drishya.

Elton shrugged. "I don't know," he said slowly, narrowing his eyes suspiciously. "In the end he never showed up. We waited for hours. Dad said that he was probably unbelievably busy coming up with cool inventions. We've been using the statue as a communal dressing-gown hanger ever since." Elton held up the microchip again. "Still, I don't mind because Dad can get lots of great stuff like this," he said.

"Incredible," said Drishya, staring at it. "The fastest microchip in the whole world."

Elton looked at her and snorted. "Er, this just in, it's actually the second fastest," he said. "Dad says that Noel Skum has just developed something much more powerful than the SKUM9. It's called the SKUM10 and they're putting it into some brand-new machines that they've been developing."

"Wow," said Drishya again, who was in such a trance that she loosened her grip on the tray, ever so slightly. "The second fastest microchip in the whole world, that's amazi—"

But before Drishya could finish her sentence about the awesomeness of the SKUM9 microchip, she felt the plate loaded with veggie ravioli slide forwards on her tray. It would have just fallen on the floor if Drishya hadn't tried to adjust the tray in a crazy, last-ditch attempt to stop any spillage.

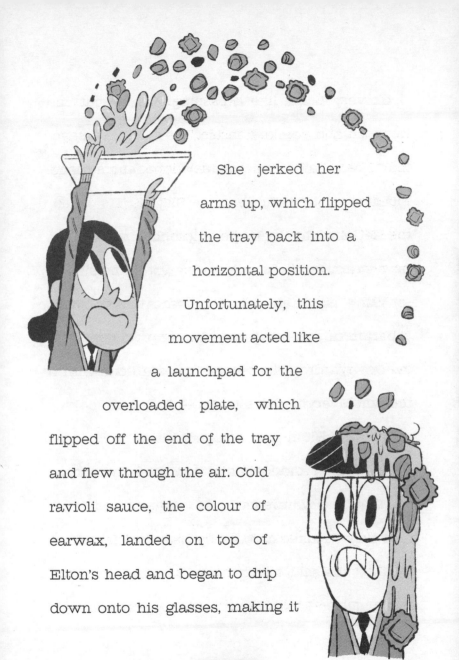

She jerked her arms up, which flipped the tray back into a horizontal position. Unfortunately, this movement acted like a launchpad for the overloaded plate, which flipped off the end of the tray and flew through the air. Cold ravioli sauce, the colour of earwax, landed on top of Elton's head and began to drip down onto his glasses, making it look very much like a passing gigantic cat had stopped and vomited on him.

"Woah," said Commodore, looking at his friend. "That is totally not rad."

He carefully took the microchip from Elton and examined it. "It's okay, I've got it," he sighed, shaking his head. "No damage. All cool. Well, apart from you being covered in food, I guess."

Drishya dropped her tray on the floor with a clatter. Everyone in the whole hall was looking at her and Elton's gunk-covered face.

He turned and looked at her. "W-why did you do that?" he whimpered.

Drishya looked horrified by what had happened. "Elton," she said, trying to scrape some ravioli off his shoulder. "I'm so sorry. I didn't mean to do that."

Drishya felt her body lurch forwards as Brianna slapped her on the back.

"That was so VE-SOME!" she shrieked, wiping tears of laughter out of her eyes. "We so thought you weren't going to do it."

"But you, like, totally, like, did it," added Janet.

"Elton, I'm really sorry," said Drishya again.

But before Elton could say anything, Brianna put her arm around Drishya's shoulder and the Dream Squad led her out of the lunch hall and into the playground.

THERE'S NO SUCH THING AS A FREE LUNCH (EVEN WHEN IT'S FREE)

The sun had long since vanished beneath the horizon and darkness had wrapped its shawl around Dreary Inkling. But, high on the twenty-seventh floor of Skum Industries 2000 HQ, a light still burned in the biggest office in the building. Noel Skum sat in an enormous leather swivel-chair, wriggling his feet that didn't even touch the ground. He stared at his computer screen and an email he was writing.

FROM: Noel Skum, Skum Industries 2000

TO: Mrs Tittering, Dreary Inkling Primary School

Dear Mrs Tittering,

Thank you for your recent enquiry into Skum Industries 2000's brand-new range of V-850 smart vending machines. We have taken the greatest care to design a new breed of vending machine that is as harmless to the environment as possible. For example, the range of SkumSnax that the machines dispense are completely eco-friendly, and made using one hundred per cent organic ingredients. The V-850 also comes with its own trash collecting system, which stores old wrappers and cans. This will be collected by one of my team of trained trash technicians and taken off the school premises for no extra cost. You can say goodbye to stinky bins and horrid bin juice.

In addition, I am pleased to inform you that Skum Industries 2000 will give you your first supply of SkumSnax for free. You will only pay when the first batch has run out.

If you would like to proceed with an order then please let me know as soon as possible. Dreary Inkling Primary School could be Skum-ready by Monday morning.

Yours sincerely,

Noel Skum

Noel Skum hit send and began pushing himself around and around in his chair while he waited.

He didn't have to wait for very long, as a few minutes later, his email pinged with a reply. He stopped spinning and stared at the screen.

FROM: Mrs Tittering, Dreary Inkling Primary School
TO: Noel Skum, Skum Industries 2000

Dear Mr Skum,

Thank you for your email. Your vending machines sound wonderful and just the thing our school needs. We would love three of them, please. I can't believe that you just give away the first supply of snacks and drinks. It's very kind. It's like you're giving us free lunches.

Yours,

Elvira Tittering

Noel Skum tapped his fingers together as he read Mrs Tittering's email and smiled. Not a kind smile but a strange, awful smile that spread across his face like an infection.

"Oh, my dear Mrs Tittering," he said, stroking his wig. "Don't you know that there's no such thing as a free lunch?"

SATURDAY

THE BATTLE BOTTOM

Drishya watched as sparks exploded in front of her. The air felt hot and dangerous as burning lights flashed before her eyes.

"Magic," she muttered, as more sparks fizzed and crackled before falling harmlessly to the floor.

She put the welding wand back in its holder and pushed a large safety mask up from her face. She had begun welding last year, when she had built the Legendary Slayer. Her mum had insisted that she had proper lessons from a professional so that she would know how to be safe. So, every Thursday night, Drishya had gone along to the local college and completed a Beginners' Guide to Welding course. She had been the youngest person there but had come top of the class.

Drishya looked at the metal dome that made up the tortoise-like shell on the back of her battle bot. She smiled at her handiwork.

"Phase one of Project G.E.O.F.F. complete," she said. "Now, I just need to sort the rest of you out before Friday. Oh, and somehow find a team."

She looked at the battle bot's circuitry that lay on the workbench. The kit she had really wanted was way too expensive so her mum had got her some bits and pieces from her work. It was alright but Drishya knew that if she wanted to stand a chance at ROBOCALYPSE, she'd have to find a way of making G.E.O.F.F. much more powerful.

"If only I had one of those SKUM9s," she said to herself. "Maybe I could persuade Elton to give me his?"

Then she remembered that the last time she had seen Elton he'd been sitting in class wearing his swimming trunks and an arts and crafts apron because his clothes were covered in vegetarian ravioli.

"Then again, perhaps not." She shuddered.

Drishya put the welding mask on the workbench as the door to the garage opened. A tiny woman with small round glasses and hair like spun steel bustled into the room.

"Where's my sweet little jalebi?" she said.

Drishya smiled and ran over to her grandma, who she towered over, and gave her a huge hug.

"Hi, Nani Ji."

Nani Ji came over every Saturday to spend the day with Drishya and her family. This was the way of things and had happened for as long as Drishya could remember.

Even though Nani Ji was small and old, her grip was fierce.

"Let me look at you," she said, peering at Drishya through the spectacles that perched on her nose. She stared at Drishya's greasy clothes. "What is this? Who are you? This face is too dirty to be my granddaughter's. What have you done with my Drishya?"

Nani Ji pursed her lips so tightly that Drishya worried that she might accidentally suck in her entire face.

"But it is me, Nani Ji," she said, taking her hair out of an elastic band and letting it tumble over her shoulders.

Nani Ji took a handkerchief out of her pocket, spat on it and rubbed a patch of grease off Drishya's face.

"Oh my goodness," she said, her mouth almost breaking into a smile. "There she is, underneath all that filth and sludge. I can see her now. Why did you do this to yourself?"

Drishya smiled. "I'm making a battle bot," she said.

"A whatty what?" spluttered Nani Ji.

"A battle bot," said Drishya. "It's a sort of robot. Look, it's over here."

Nani Ji adjusted her glasses and peered at G.E.O.F.F. "What does it do?" she asked.

"Well," said Drishya. "It's supposed to destroy other robots."

Nani Ji sighed a big sigh. "I suppose it's for that TV show you like so much, what is it? Roboty Clips or something?"

Drishya laughed. "**ROBOCALYPSE**, Nani Ji," she said.

Nani Ji shook her head. "In my day we used to go outside and fill our lungs with fresh air," she said. "Not stay indoors building things to smash other things." She nervously touched G.E.O.F.F.'s shell like it was going to give her an electric shock. "This technology is too much. I didn't have robots and computers to play with when I was your age, but I was happy. Now, I come here on a lovely sunny day and I find my granddaughter covered in gunk because she wants to stay inside a garage all day long."

Drishya smiled. "Technology is good, Nani Ji," she said.

Nani Ji sighed again. "That is what everyone keeps telling me," she said. "Last week, your father told me that he had bought me a new tablet. I told him, I have enough tablets already. I take them for my heart and for my knees. Then he gives me this." Nani Ji opened up her handbag and pulled out a handheld device the size of a book. "I mean, how am I supposed to swallow this?" she said. "I can't even break it in half."

Drishya shook her head. "You don't have to swallow it. It's a computer. You can browse the internet on it, watch movies on it; you never know, you might even like it."

Nani Ji snorted like she didn't believe that for a second. "So, this battle bottom of yours," she said, putting her tablet back in her handbag. "It will destroy other robots, right?"

"It's a battle BOT," laughed Drishya. "And it's supposed to destroy other robots but I'm worried that it might be a bit small. It could be a bit weak."

Nani Ji turned and looked at Drishya. "I am small," she said. "You think that I'm weak?"

Drishya was horrified. Her grandma might have been tiny but she was the toughest person Drishya knew. There was a family rumour that, as a young woman, Nani Ji had been the undefeated arm-wrestling champion of Mumbai.

"Oh, no, no, Nani Ji, not at all," stammered Drishya. "It's just that I-I-I—"

Nani Ji smiled and leaned closer to Drishya. "Being small does not mean you are weak," she whispered. "When you fight, you fight with this," she tapped her head, "and with this," she tapped her heart. "Robots are no different. Use the size of your botty bot to your advantage. Small is nimble. Small is speedy. And if all else fails, hit them hard when they're not looking." Nani Ji smiled and patted Drishya on her arm. "Now then," she said. "You go and get washed."

"Okay, okay, Nani Ji," said Drishya. "I've just finished in here anyway."

Nani Ji reached up and pinched Drishya's cheek with her bony fingers. Her grip was vice tight. "Good girl, and after you're clean, I need you to go to the shops and get some flour," she said, pushing a two-pound coin into Drishya's hand.

"Sure thing, Nani Ji," said Drishya.

"You mother will be back from work in an hour and I said I'd make some chapatis for her."

Drishya's eyes lit up at the thought of her Nani Ji's warm chapatis, straight from the stove.

"Also," said Nani Ji, holding up her tablet, "I can't find the rolling pin. Perhaps I shall use this to flatten the chapatis instead. At least then it will be of some use."

MONSTER TRUCK

Drishya was almost at the shop when she heard her name being shouted from somewhere across the high street.

"Drishya!"

She stopped and looked around but couldn't see anyone at all.

"Drishya!" shouted the voice again. "Drishya, over here! Look down!"

Across the road was a line of cones surrounding

a huge hole that had been dug into the pavement. And, as Drishya looked, a familiar head popped up from inside the hole.

Drishya waved and carefully crossed the road. "Hi, Mum," she said. "How's it going?"

Drishya squatted down by the side of the hole and looked in. It was enormous and jam-packed full of cables. A man in a hard hat was holding a big bunch of multicoloured wires in one hand and a small device in the other. He shook his head and sucked his teeth very loudly.

"Well, it's much worse than we thought," said

Drishya's mum. "It's going to take us quite a while to sort it out. Did your father remember to pick up Nani Ji?"

Drishya nodded. "He remembered to put some trousers on too," she said.

Drishya's mum smiled as a loud beeping sound came from the small device the man was holding. He held it up to show Drishya's mum the readout. Her face immediately changed to a frown.

"Oh dear, that's not good," she said to the man, before turning back to Drishya. "Look, love, I've got to get on. I'll see you later."

"Okay, Mum," said Drishya, standing up as her mum began chatting worriedly to the man. "See you."

Drishya crossed back over the road and walked

towards the shop. She was just about to go inside when Elton Gweek and Commodore Sinclair opened the door and walked out. Commodore was wearing cut-off jeans, flip-flops and a hoodie, and under his arm he was carrying a remote-controlled truck. Elton had a T-shirt with the words *I'm A Chess Nut* written on it in large letters. Drishya let out a little laugh-snort at the joke. The boys stopped and looked at her. Elton's face immediately crumpled in horror.

"Er, hi," said Drishya.

Elton's face flushed red and he looked like he wanted to say something but instead he put his head down and hurried past. Commodore followed close behind.

"Wait," said Drishya, rushing after them. "I'm really, really sorry about what happened yesterday. I never meant for you to get covered in food."

Elton stopped and turned around. "You and Brianna had a pretty good laugh about it," he said, quietly.

"I wasn't laughing," said Drishya. "I felt terrible. I never wanted it to happen, honestly."

Commodore looked at her. He put down his truck and began driving it around the pavement. It slalomed around stones and litter with incredible speed and precision.

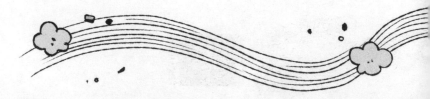

"Word in the playground is that you're joining the Dream Squad," he said, without looking up from his remote control.

"I-I'm not," said Drishya. "They want me to join because of my cardigan."

She paused. Commodore's truck spun around her legs three times then zipped off down the pavement.

"It's a long story," she added. "But they wanted me to do a horrible initiation."

Elton narrowed his eyes. "What initiation?"

"They wanted me to tip my food all over you," said Drishya.

Elton narrowed his eyes even more until they were, technically, shut. "Er, this just in," he said. "You did tip your food all over me."

"I know, but it was an accident," said Drishya. "I was distracted by your SKUM9 and the Noel Skum story, and the tray just sort of fell out of my hands and you ended up getting covered. I don't want to join the Dream Squad. I'm really, really, really, really sorry."

Elton sighed. "It's okay," he said, un-narrowing his eyes a little bit. "I suppose."

Drishya looked down and noticed that Elton was holding a piece of paper that had the word **ROBOCALYPSE** in big letters at the top.

"What's that?" she said, pointing at the piece of paper.

Elton glanced at it. "Oh, it's a ticket for **ROBOCALYPSE**," he said. "You know, the TV show. It's coming to Dreary Inkling on Friday and we're going to be in the audience. Front row seats."

"You guys like **ROBOCALYPSE**?" said Drishya. "It's my favourite TV show, ever. I was going to enter it, if I could get a team together."

A brilliant idea suddenly struck Drishya.

"Wait," she said. "Would you guys like to be in a team together?"

Elton and Commodore looked at each other, eyebrows raised.

"A team? With you?" said Elton. "After what you did yesterday?"

"I told you, I'm really sorry about that," she said. "Take a look at this."

Drishya reached down and opened a secret pocket halfway down her trouser leg. She pulled out a piece of paper and slowly unfolded it. It was one of her blueprints for G.E.O.F.F.

"Oh man, that's awesome," said Commodore. "Did you design this?"

Drishya nodded. "Yeah," she said. "I even started building some of it this morning but..." She paused.

"What?" said Elton.

"Well," she said, "I'm worried that it's a bit slow and underpowered. Mum got me some circuits from her work but they're pretty basic. I just feel that it needs something else, something that will make it much more powerful."

Commodore's eyes lit up. He nudged Elton and made a face, like he was trying to communicate something important that he didn't want to say out loud. Elton stared at Commodore like he didn't think the silent-but-important thing was a very good idea. But then, Commodore squinted at Elton, like he was trying to get Elton to reconsider the silent-but-important thing. Eventually, Elton sighed and shrugged like he still had reservations but that, in principle, he agreed to the silent-but-important thing. The pair turned and looked at Drishya.

"Well, I suppose you could use the SCUM9 microchip," said Elton.

"Really?" said Drishya.

"I guess, you know, if we were part of a team, it'd be acceptable," said Elton.

Drishya looked at him. "Well," she said. "Are you guys in?"

Elton looked at Commodore. They nodded at

each other and smiled.

"This just in," said Elton. "We would like very much to be in a **ROBOCALYPSE** team with you."

"That's brilliant," said Drishya and high-fived Commodore. She tried to high-five Elton too but it didn't really work because Elton hadn't ever felt very comfortable high-fiving people so they just shook hands instead.

Commodore made his truck do a super-fast 720 degree spin before speeding it back around a hole in the pavement and skidding it to a stop, right by his feet.

"And if you need a driver, I'm your dude," he said, flicking his hair out of his eyes.

Drishya couldn't believe it. She had found her team for **ROBOCALYPSE**. She was so happy. But as she stood smiling and chatting with Elton and Commodore about their favourite **ROBOCALYPSE** robots, the three of them became aware of a deep rumbling noise that was coming down the street. They all turned and watched, open-mouthed, as an enormous, gleaming truck growled along Dreary Inkling High Street and turned down Wildhack Lane. The truck had the words SKUM INDUSTRIES 2000 emblazoned on the side.

"What was that?" said Elton.

"Come on," said Drishya. "Let's see where it's going!"

The three of them sprinted after the truck. As they turned onto Wildhack Lane they could see it up ahead, turning down Bradbury Road.

"Quick," shouted Drishya, her long legs running faster than either Elton or Commodore could manage.

When they reached the corner of Bradbury Road they stopped and stared as something happened that they would never have dreamed could happen in a hundred billion years. The Skum Industries 2000 truck stopped outside Dreary Inkling Primary School and reversed into the playground.

MONDAY

NOEL SKUM

The door to the school hall crashed open and Drishya raced in. She was late and everybody turned to stare at her as she paused, sweating and panting, and scanned the room for a place to sit.

She was late because her mum had gone out early again. The electrical problem on the high street was getting worse and her crew were going to have to dig up even more of the road. Drishya's dad had been in a terrible flap, again, and had spent twenty minutes panicking that he couldn't find his glasses, until Drishya had pointed out that he didn't have any glasses because he had perfect eyesight. Then they'd got stuck in a bad traffic jam on their way to school and Drishya's dad had got really frustrated and said that whoever caused it was "a stupid stinking bag of plops". But then Drishya reminded him that it was probably her mum who had caused the traffic jam because she was digging up the road and her dad went quiet for a long time, apart from grinding his teeth really loudly.

Drishya looked around the hall. All the places on the Year Six bench had been taken. She saw Brianna waving at her and beckoning her to go over. Janet and Kimberley were trying to budge

Eddie Splott out of the way to make space for Drishya on the bench, but Eddie wasn't going anywhere. It was one of the golden rules of Year Six that when you had a space on the bench, you guarded it with your life. Then, Drishya spotted Elton and Commodore sitting together on the floor. There was a tiny space next to them so Drishya made her way over. There was a powerful, weird energy buzzing in the hall, with lots of excited whispers fluttering around and

pockets of nervous, giggling laughter. It did not feel like a usual Monday morning at all.

"Hi, guys," she said, sitting down next to Commodore, whose long hair looked so much like a bird's nest that Drishya was sure he must have styled it that way on purpose.

"Oh, hi," he said, sticking his finger through a hole in the knee of his trousers.

"What's that?" said Drishya, pointing to something on the stage that was covered in a big black cloth.

"Oh yeah, we were just chatting about that," said Commodore. "We were thinking that it was maybe something that the truck delivered on Saturday?"

Drishya nodded. "Makes sense," she said.

Elton cleared his throat. "Drishya," he said, "I've been putting some thought into our team name for **ROBOCALYPSE**. I have come up with something that I think will be perfect."

Drishya looked at him, surprised. "Oh, right," she said. "What have you got?"

Elton pushed up his glasses. "Well, there are three of us, are there not?" he said.

Drishya nodded. "Yes," she said.

"And we each bring a different skill, or skills, to the team, do we not?"

Drishya nodded again. "Er, yes," she said. "You've got access to great hardware, I'm good at building the bots, and Commodore is an expert driver."

Drishya and Commodore high-fived.

"Correct," said Elton. "So, why don't we call ourselves the 'Three People Whose Individual Talents Have Come Together to Make a Great Team' Team?"

Drishya looked at Commodore and back at Elton.

"Er, it's great," she said. "But it might be a bit of a mouthful."

"Ooh, ooh," said Commodore excitedly. "Maybe we should just call ourselves 'Triple Threat'."

"Triple Threat?" said Drishya. "I love it!"

A hush suddenly fell across the hall. Mrs

Tittering strode through the doors at the back followed by a very small man who scurried along, wearing a very obvious wig and a pair of large black sunglasses. There was something familiar about him. He was wearing an overcoat that covered his body but Drishya caught a glimpse of a pair of pristine, white cowboy boots.

Drishya's breathing suddenly began to get quicker. "O-oh, m-my, g-gosh," she stammered quietly, almost too excited to speak.

When Mrs Tittering and the strange man got onto the stage, Mrs Tittering took off her small half-moon glasses and let them hang from her neck on a gold chain.

"Good morning, children," she said.

"Good mor-ning, Mis-sus Ti-tter-ing, good

mor-ning, ev-ery-bod-y," said the whole school, at the same time, in a way that sounded like each and every one of them was a robot whose batteries were about to die.

"Now, children," continued Mrs Tittering, towering over the strange man. "We have a very exciting visitor here this morning. Someone who is so important that he had to come in disguise."

"I-it's h-him," stuttered Drishya, nudging Elton and Commodore. "I-it's r-really h-him."

Mrs Tittering smiled. "The one and only..."

The man standing next to Mrs Tittering threw off his overcoat to reveal his trademark black all-in-one jumpsuit with matching cape attachment.

"Dreary Inkling's very own billionaire, Noel Skum!"

A gasp of shock and excitement burst out of the mouths of everyone in the school hall as Noel Skum whipped off his sunglasses to reveal his small dark eyes, then pulled off his obvious wig to reveal another obvious wig that perched on top of his head like a dead gerbil.

Drishya couldn't contain her excitement and let out a little shriek.

"Hello! Hello! Hello!" he shouted, and ran around the stage waving his arms around like his armpits were on fire.

"Welcome to Dreary Inkling Primary, Mr Skum," said Mrs Tittering, smiling again. "I understand that you have a, er, little surprise for us this morning."

Noel Skum suddenly stopped running around

the stage and stared at Mrs Tittering.

"Little?" he shouted. "Little? What do you mean little? Are you saying that I'm little? That I'm short?"

Mrs Tittering looked shocked. "Er, no, not at all," she said. "It was just a figure of speech."

Noel Skum continued to stare at Mrs Tittering. "Good," he said. "Because I'm not at all little."

Mrs Tittering smiled nervously. "Okay," she said, after an awkward silence. "Well why don't you tell us about your big surprise?"

Noel Skum's face suddenly cracked into a smile and he walked over to the large object on the stage, grabbing a corner of the black cloth.

"Behold," he said, pulling the cloth away to reveal a huge, silver vending machine that had a screen on its front where two green, digital eyes blinked and looked around. "Feast your eyes on the newest and most delicious snacks that money can buy. I give you...SkumSnax."

Another huge gasp echoed around the hall. The vending machine was wearing a large sash around its body that said NEW SKUMSNAX SOLD HERE. And behind the large pane of glass at the front of the vending machine were row upon row of green snack bags with glinting, golden writing.

Noel Skum stared out at his audience, his eyes blazing. "Welcome to the future of lunch," he said.

THE FUTURE OF LUNCH

Drishya sat in stunned silence, staring at Noel Skum, scarcely able to believe that her hero was in the hall of her school. It was abso-blummin'-incredopants.

Noel Skum stood on the stage, his cape attachment fluttering slightly in a draught, wearing a smile of such smug self-satisfaction, that he looked like someone who had just managed to do a really stinky fart and blame it on a passing dog.

"You will be able to buy all three delicious and BRAND-NEW flavours of SkumSnax in one of these vending machines," he said.

"I can't believe the school's getting vending machines," whispered Commodore, nudging Drishya and Elton. "This is SO brilliant."

Elton nodded. "We'll never have to eat horrible broccoli again," he said.

"Sssshhhhhh," said Drishya. "What's that he's got?"

She was looking at a remote control that Noel Skum had pulled out of his pocket.

"This is no ordinary vending machine," he said. "This is one of the new generation of Skum Industries V-850 vending machines. The most advanced vending machines in the whole world."

He pushed a button on the remote control.

"The fuuuu-tuuuure of luuuuuunch," sang the vending machine.

"Amazing," said Drishya, shaking her head in disbelief.

Noel Skum walked around the V-850 and pulled a coin out of his pocket. "First," he said, "you take a one-pound coin..." He paused dramatically. "And you throw it away, because the V-850 does not need coins." Noel Skum flung the coin off the stage, not even caring to look where it went.

"GASP," said the room.

"OW!" said Rory Bummlers, from Year Three, as the coin bounced off his head.

"Next," shrieked Noel Skum, "you take a five-pound, or a ten-pound note." He grabbed a wallet out of his back pocket and held it up. "Then you throw them away as well because the V-850 does not need notes either," he yelled, throwing his wallet off the stage.

"GASP," said the room, again.

"OW!" said Rory Bummlers again, who had been so busy rubbing his head from the coin that he hadn't been watching Noel Skum throw the wallet, which had also hit him on the head. Rory sat rubbing his head and staring at Noel Skum, who was now holding another, smaller wallet.

"The V-850 does not need credit cards either," Noel Skum said, taking credit card after credit card out of the wallet and flicking them offstage like they were ninja death stars.

This time Rory was watching and managed to dodge all the cards. Well, he thought he had, because he thought he'd seen Noel Skum throw three credit cards but actually, Noel Skum had thrown four credit cards and the last one took Rory by surprise and hit him on the head.

"GASP," said the room.

"OW!" said Rory, who jumped up and ran out of the hall crying.

Noel Skum stood with his legs far apart and his hands on

his hips. "No," he said. "The V-850 needs no money of any kind. The V-850 just needs your eyes."

Noel Skum walked over to the vending machine and stood facing the two blinking, green eyes. As he did, a kind of red laser beam shot out of the machine and moved around his face. Eventually the beam scanned his eyes and the vending machine made a happy "pinging" sound.

"Good morning, Mr Skum, and how can I help you today?" said the V-850 in a calm, monotone voice.

Another gasp of astonishment erupted in the school hall.

"It can speak!" said Drishya looking at Elton and Commodore. "That vending machine has got artificial intelligence."

Noel Skum turned to face his audience. "Each of these state-of-the-art vending machines is fully stocked with all three flavours of SkumSnax, including the brand-new flavour, CHOCOLATEY BEEF."

Drishya turned and looked at Commodore and Elton. "Chocolatey beef," she whispered. "That sounds awful."

On the stage, Noel Skum addressed the vending machine. "What do you think of the new SkumSnax?" he said.

The V-850's eyes blinked. "SkumSnax are the most delicious snack in the whole world," it said in its monotone voice.

"Exactly," said Noel Skum. "Now, give me a packet of incredible, new chocolatey beef

SkumSnax."

The V-850 blinked and with a whooshing sound, a packet of SkumSnax fell into its large dispensing slot. Then a robotic arm whirred out of the side of the vending machine, grabbed the snacks and handed them to Noel Skum.

"Mmmmm, they look amazing," he said, taking them from the V-850.

But instead of eating the SkumSnax, Drishya noticed that he put them down on a chair, and she thought she saw a slight wrinkle of his nose.

Mrs Tittering turned and addressed the school. "Well, thank you, Mr Skum," she said. "Now then, there are three of Mr Skum's wonderful vending machines in the school and I'll be coming round this morning to every class and scanning everyone's eyeballs so you'll be able to use the machines at break-time. Your unique eyeball pattern will be linked to an account that we've set up for each of you. Your parents will need to put some money in the account for you to use, although the first supply of SkumSnax has been very generously given to us by Mr Skum."

Everyone cheered at the news of free snacks as Mrs Tittering and Noel Skum left the stage.

"This is so cool," said Commodore, trying to make himself heard over the excited chatter as everyone left the school hall and made their way to their classrooms. "Those vending machines look awesome."

Drishya's mind was in a whirl. The vending machines in her school might be the most advanced robots in the history of the world. It was like they could think for themselves, almost as if they were human. It was unbelievable. She was just thinking about what the insides of such a machine might look like when she felt someone tugging at her arm. She turned around and saw

Brianna and the other members of the Dream Squad just behind her.

"We'll do initiation number two today," said Brianna.

"It'll be like a totally ve-some initiation," said Janet.

"V v v ve-some," added Kimberley.

And the three members of the Dream Squad charged past her to get their bags from the cloakroom.

"The fuuuu-tuuuure of luuuuuunch," sang the vending machine as Drishya passed it on her way out of the hall.

She turned and watched, her eyes wide with amazement, as a robotic arm emerged from the vending machine and grabbed the packet of

SkumSnax that Noel Skum had put on the chair.

"Waste retrieval and disposal," said the V-850 in its calm, monotone voice as the robotic arm and the bag disappeared inside the body of the machine.

THE AWESOMENESS OF VENDING MACHINES

Throughout the morning, the excitement about the new vending machines grew and grew and grew. It was like the school was a bottle of fizzy drink that someone had shaken up and that any minute was going to explode. By morning break, every pupil in the school had had their retinas scanned and their vending accounts opened and ready for use. As soon as the break bell buzzed, classrooms emptied in record time as everyone raced to the one fully-installed vending machine.

"One at a time," screamed Mrs Tittering, who was looking even more flustered than usual as she and the music teacher, Mr Jagger, tried to hold back the surging horde of kids from the machine. "This is the only vending machine up and running at the moment so please be patient."

Drishya, Elton and Commodore were nearly at the back of the line.

"You know you were saying about G.E.O.F.F. being a bit slow," said Commodore, while they waited.

Drishya nodded.

"Well," he continued, "I've got a rad remote-controlled car that my mum wants me to throw away because it's totally smashed up. It was super-fast."

Drishya looked at him, confused. "So?"

"Well," said Commodore. "The car might be broken but the wheel-base and the motor still work perfectly. So..."

"We could attach the wheel-base to G.E.O.F.F.," said Drishya, finishing off the thought.

"That's BRILLIANT!" she said.

"Triple Threat," said Commodore, holding the middle three fingers of his right hand up and wiping them in front of his eyes.

Drishya was about to try the new Triple Threat sign herself when she saw Brianna, Kimberley and Janet walking towards them, chatting and laughing. Drishya ducked behind Elton.

"Dream Squad," she whispered.

"Have they seen me?"

Elton turned around and saw that the girls had stopped and were talking to each other, just outside the cloakrooms. They didn't look over.

"That's a negative," he said. "We have zero eye-contact."

"Good," said Drishya. "The last thing I need is another initiation, and we're never going to get to the front of the queue at this rate. Let's go outside."

Elton and Commodore nodded and the trio headed away from the Dream Squad, chatting excitedly about Triple Threat and **ROBOCALYPSE**. As they neared the door to go outside, Drishya spotted something down the corridor that led to the library.

"Look," she said. "Another machine is being installed."

Sure enough, down the corridor, a woman wearing brown Skum Industries 2000 overalls was using a remote control to wheel the vending machine into its place against a wall. Drishya,

Elton and Commodore went to have a closer look. They could see that a metal shutter was pulled down over the front of the machine's body with the words "SORRY I AM CLOSED" written on it in large letters

The woman in the brown overalls stood and looked at the vending machine. "V-850," she said. "Wake up and find your position. Do you read me?"

The metal shutter automatically rolled up, revealing the vending machine's green digital eyes.

"Affirmative, Davina," it said in its calm monotone voice. "I read you."

Then the vending machine blinked and its eyes began to rotate, like it was looking around the corridor.

"That's so cool," said Drishya.

The vending machine looked at Drishya. Its eyes were two small green circles inside two larger green rings, with a green line above each of them for eyebrows. Drishya knew they were just lights on a digital screen but somehow, they seemed so real, so alive.

"Thank you," it said.

Drishya gasped.

"OMG," said Commodore. "That's AMAZING!"

Davina smiled at them. "These new vending machines are very responsive to humans," she said. "Mr Skum has been working on them for months. It's all thanks to an incredibly powerful microchip inside the vending machine. It's the most powerful chip in the world. Look."

Davina handed Drishya an operating manual open at a page showing off a bright orange microchip with lots of little black legs.

"It says it's a SKUM10 microchip," said Drishya, reading from the manual.

"That's the one Dad told me about," said Elton.

They watched as the V-850 finished backing itself against the wall.

"Is it battery powered?" said Drishya.

"It has a limited battery life," said Davina, "so we'll be plugging it into the mains."

She walked over to the V-850, unwound a plug on a lead that had been hidden on the side of the machine, and plugged it into the wall.

"Diagnostic check," she said.

The V-850 blinked. "All systems normal,

Davina," said the vending machine. "It feels good to be awake again. Advanced battery cells will recharge whilst on mains electricity."

Davina turned the remote control off. "Well, it's all ready to use. Enjoy," she said and walked off down the hall, whistling to herself.

Drishya looked at Commodore and Elton and smiled. "Anyone hungry?" she said, walking up to the machine.

Drishya stood facing the two blinking eyes. The red laser they had seen earlier shot out of the machine and began scanning her face.

"What does it feel like?" asked Elton.

"Dunno," said Drishya. "It doesn't feel like anything really, it's just a teeny bit warm."

The V-850 stopped scanning and the two eyes

blinked. "Good morning, Drishya Samode," it said. "How can I be of assistance?"

Drishya smiled. "I'd like a packet of SkumSnax, please."

The machine blinked. "Which flavour would you like?" said the V-850. "There are three exciting new flavours, cheese and pickled egg flavour, banana and prawn flavour, and chocolatey beef flavour."

"Er, cheese and pickled egg flavour, please,"
said Drishya.

Elton and Commodore did the three-fingered
Triple Threat sign
in giddy anticipation
of getting something
out of the vending
machine.

The machine blinked again and suddenly a
green packet fell into the dispensing slot. A robot
arm popped out of the side of the machine,
grabbed the bag of cheese and pickled egg
SkumSnax and held them up to Drishya.

"That is RAD," said Commodore.

"Er, this just in," said Elton. "It's the raddest
thing EVER!"

Drishya took the packet from the vending machine's arm. Her hands trembled ever so slightly as she carefully opened up the bag to reveal the perfectly circular, crisp-like SkumSnax. She closed her eyes, held the opened packet up to her nose and sniffed in the aroma.

"Urgh!" she said.

"What?" asked Elton.

"There's something funny about them," said Drishya. "Like they've gone off, or something."

"NEGATIVE."

Drishya turned and saw that the vending machine was looking at her, frowning.

"No SkumSnax ever go off, they are perfect snacks," it said. "SkumSnax are made from organic ingredients. Your nose must be faulty."

Drishya was about to say something when the door at the end of the corridor flew open and in ran Eddie Splott and Tom Boosbeck. Eddie snatched the SkumSnax from her and, grabbing handfuls of the savoury circles, shovelled them into his mouth.

"These things are amazing," he said, spitting SkumSnax crumbs over the floor as he spoke.

Before anyone knew what had happened, Eddie had finished the packet, crumpled the bag up into a ball and thrown it at the vending machine. Then he and Tom ran off, hooting with laughter.

"Idiot," said Elton, as the end-of-break bell buzzed.

The V-850 blinked twice and the robotic arm

picked up the empty packet of SkumSnax.

"Waste retrieval and disposal," it said, as the robotic arm and rubbish disappeared inside its body.

"Come on," said Drishya. "Let's go."

As she, Commodore and Elton headed back to their classroom, the V-850's green eyes blinked twice and turned red, watching them as they left. Then the red eyes blinked again and turned back to green.

"The fuuuu-tuuuure of luuuuuunch," it sang.

DEVIOUS FLAVOUR-MAKING

Mrs Tittering waved goodbye to Noel Skum and watched as he walked through the school playground and got into his Skum Industries 2000 self-driving hovercar. The school corridors were quiet as everyone was in class. She was about to go into her office, where she planned to put her feet up and have her usual mid-morning snooze, when she heard a clunking and clattering noise coming from around the corner.

"That's funny," she said, and went to investigate.

But when Mrs Tittering turned the corner there was no sign of anything strange at all. She could see the photocopier, a couple of pot plants and one of the new vending machines that was stationed right outside the staff room.

"I must be imagining things," she said, before heading back to her office.

Once inside, she locked the door and lay down on her large sofa. She put her hand out and reached underneath for her fluffy eye mask.

"Urgh!" she said, and snatched her hand back up. It was covered in something green and slimy that had been on her floor. She sniffed her fingers and pulled a face. "Smells like bins," she said wiping her hand on the sofa to get rid of the strange liquid. "Disgusting."

Mrs Tittering got up and looked around for her eye mask but it was nowhere to be seen. It had simply vanished.

Meanwhile, Noel Skum's car hovered down the road outside. Inside the car, Noel Skum had put his seat into its most reclined position and had activated "massage mode". He thought he would try and relax on his way back to the office. He closed his eyes and breathed out slowly, enjoying this moment of calm.

PING PING PING

"Call coming in from Skum HQ," said the car.

Noel Skum snorted. "ANSWER!" he yelled.

A face appeared on the dashboard of the car and a voice crackled through the surround-sound car speakers.

"Er, hello? Er, Mr Skum, can you hear me? It's Alan from the office."

Noel Skum stared at the screen.

"Er, Alan Remnant," prompted Alan. "Er, your assistant."

Noel Skum rolled his eyes. "I can hear you and see you, you disgusting worm-faced sniveller,"

he growled. "What do you want?"

"Er, well, Mr Skum," said Alan, who was beginning to sweat a little. "I've been crunching some numbers..."

Noel Skum sighed.

"...And, er, it's just that I, er, think that you might have made a mistake."

Alan went quiet.

The line crackled.

Noel Skum sat upright in his chair and looked at the image of Alan's face like he was trying to kill Alan with his eyes.

"I?" he said slowly. "Made a mistake?"

Alan nodded. "Er, well, er, yes," he stuttered.

"You think that Noel Skum, billionaire and winner of the prestigious Dreary Inkling Sneer of the Year for the last three years, has made a mistake?" said Noel Skum.

Alan gulped. "Well, er, Mr Skum, it's just the payment scheme on the vending machines. As of this morning, you have a total of one hundred machines at various locations around the country."

"Yes?" said Noel Skum.

"Well, I've just been told that you're not going to be charging anyone for the first supply of the new SkumSnax."

"Yes?" said Noel Skum. "And?"

Alan was sweating quite a lot now.

"Er, well, sir, that's over one hundred thousand

pounds worth of SkumSnax products that you're just giving away. Er, for free." Alan paused and mopped his sweaty face with a hankie.

"SILENCE!" screeched Noel Skum.

The line crackled.

"Oh, you had already finished, hadn't you?"

Alan nodded meekly.

"Well in that case, REMAIN SILENT!" screamed Noel Skum. "You are a gigantic poo-poo-head numbskull and I should fire you immediately."

Noel Skum clicked a button and his seat whirred back into an upright position. "There are two things you need to know about SkumSnax," he said. "Firstly, they have taken me five years of devious flavour-making to develop. I have created a taste that is completely delicious to children.

Ask me how I did it. Go on, ask me."

"Er, h-how did you do it?" stammered Alan.

"Bin juice," said Noel Skum.

Alan looked blank, his mouth opening and closing like a confused goldfish.

Noel Skum sighed. "I discovered that by taking ordinary bin juice that collects in the bottom of ordinary bins and then putting it through a top-secret and highly scientific process that only I know about, I could create a super-concentrated flavour-powder, which I dust over all SkumSnax products."

Alan gagged. "You mean that SkumSnax are made using..." He paused. "...b-bin juice?"

"That is correct," said Noel Skum.

"But doesn't it taste, well...binny?" said Alan.

Noel Skum smiled. "That's the brilliant thing," he said. "Kids' taste buds don't recognize any of the garbage notes in the flavour. To almost every kid, the added bin juice makes it taste like the best thing they've ever had."

"*Almost* every kid?" said Alan.

"Yes, some vegetarian kids have developed an unusually strong sense of smell," said Noel Skum. "So, there are a few who are able to detect a binny scent. And adults find the taste repulsive, but then adults always hate things that kids like so that's not a problem."

He smiled for a moment.

"Which leads on neatly to the second thing that you need to know. Each vending machine has a recycling chute. Kids can put all their wrappers, cans, food, whatever, into the vending machines. That way, each machine will be able to create its own bin juice at absolutely no cost to us. So, once we get kids hooked on SkumSnax, we'll then start charging huge amounts for refills."

"But people will stop buying it, if it is too expensive," said Alan.

A horrible smile flickered across Noel Skum's face. "No they will not," he said. "Once someone gets a taste for my SkumSnax they will do anything to get their hands on their next bag, including paying whatever I charge them. Now go away and stop bothering me."

And with that, Noel Skum pushed a button on the armrest of his chair and Alan's face disappeared.

Noel Skum tapped his fingers together and smiled a wicked smile. "Oh, yes," he said. "All I have to do is sit back and wait for the refill orders to start rolling in."

He opened a can of orange soda and took a long swig. All this talk of bin juice had made him feel a bit queasy and he needed something to settle his tummy.

TUESDAY

A SHORTAGE
OF SNACKAGE

Drishya raced down the road towards school. She was late, again. Today, her dad had managed to get stuck in the toilet. Not stuck in the room the toilet was in, but stuck in the actual toilet.

Drishya ran through the school gates and into the playground and immediately sensed that something was wrong. She looked at her watch. It was 8.55 a.m. and yet the place was completely deserted. No one was around. No pupils, no teachers, nobody.

"That's weird," she muttered. "Where is everyone?"

It was then that she heard a distant, muffled rumble, sort of like faraway thunder. A rumble that got louder and stronger the nearer to the school building she got.

She pushed open the main door and walked into the small reception area. Mrs Fesnying, the school secretary, wasn't in her usual place in the school office. But the inner glass security door that let visitors and parents into the school was wide open.

"That's really weird," said Drishya, walking through.

As Drishya walked down the main school corridor, the noise got louder and louder. By the time she passed the music practice rooms, the sound was less like a muffled rumble of faraway thunder and more like a raging vortex of shouting and screaming. She turned a corner and stopped dead in her tracks, because she could suddenly see what was making the noise. There, along the full length of the main school corridor, was a swarming, sprawling sea of bodies, all jostling and yelling. Drishya saw Elton and Commodore standing on the table outside the Year One classroom.

"Hey," she called up to them. "What's going on?"

"Come up," shouted Commodore. "You can see more from up here."

He and Elton helped Drishya up onto the table.

"OMG," she said, shocked at what she saw.

The sprawling sea of bodies was actually a huge queue to use one of the vending machines. Mr Jagger, Ms Husk, Mrs Fesnying and Mrs Tittering were standing around the V-850, trying their hardest to hold the queue back, but it was an

impossible task. People were pushing and crying and trying anything to get their hands on some more SkumSnax.

"What's going on?" said Drishya. "It's like everyone's gone crazy."

Drishya looked at the front of the vending machine. Through the large pane of glass she could see that it was nearly empty. Luis Agueda, from her class, was hammering on the side of the vending machine because there were no more packets of chocolatey beef SkumSnax left.

"It's alright, Luis, it's just a temporary snack shortage," said Mrs Tittering, shouting to make herself heard above the din. "I'll order more this afternoon."

"It's. Not. Fair," yelled Luis, bashing the vending machine with his fists.

Drishya had never seen anything like it before, but eventually Mr Jagger managed to drag Luis, kicking and crying, away from the machine.

"I don't get it," said Drishya. "Why does everyone

want SkumSnax? They smell so weird. Have you tried them?"

Commodore and Elton shook their heads.

"Negative," said Elton. "And I don't want to try them, thank you very much. Not after your reaction to them yesterday."

The school bell buzzed for registration and the angry crowd began to disperse.

"Well, I've nearly finished building the body of G.E.O.F.F," said Drishya, stepping down from the table.

"Awesome," said Commodore. "I can't wait to take it for a spin."

"I spent the evening drawing up tactical battle plans and fighting strategies," said Elton, patting his school bag. "We could go over them at lunchtime in the canteen?"

Drishya smiled. "Sounds good," she said. "Let's meet up as soon as class finishes."

Elton nodded back over Drishya's shoulder. "Looks like your mates want to chat to you," he said.

Drishya turned and saw Brianna, Janet and Kimberley walking down the corridor. This time they had seen Drishya and were heading straight for her.

"You need to tell them you don't want to be in the Dream Squad," said Commodore.

Drishya nodded reluctantly. "I know," she said.

"Come on," said Elton, tugging Commodore's arm. "Let's leave them to it."

He glanced at Drishya. "See you in class," he

said, before he and Commodore fought their way

through the crowd.

Drishya looked back at the Dream Girls. Each

one of them scowled at her as they walked over.

They did not look happy at all.

INITIATION (2)

"We missed you yesterday," said Brianna.

Drishya smiled nervously. "Oh, er, yeah, er, sorry," she said. "I had to go to the nurse at lunch, so I wasn't around."

This was partly true. Well, the bit about Drishya not being around was true. The bit about Drishya having to go and see the nurse was a completely made-up-on-the-spot fib. Drishya had tried to avoid the Dream Squad all day and so had spent her lunch break hiding behind the coats in the Year Six cloakroom with Elton and Commodore. They'd turned the back corner into a makeshift Triple Threat HQ and spent nearly a whole hour discussing their favourite kills on **ROBOCALYPSE**.

"Well, that doesn't matter because we're going to do the second and final part of the Dream Squad initiation right now," said Brianna, smiling and adjusting her beret.

"Er, now?" said Drishya.

"Now." Brianna nodded.

"Unless you, like, totally don't want to be in the, like, Dream Squad," said Janet, flicking her hair with frightening speed.

Drishya paused and looked at Brianna and Janet and Kimberley.

"Er, well, actually, I don't think I do want—" she began, about to confess to the girls that on second, third and fourth thoughts, she didn't want to be in the Dream Squad after all.

"But, of course, EVERYONE wants to join the Dream Squad," interrupted Brianna, howling with laughter. "Because we are so totally VE-SOME."

"VE-SOME," sang Janet and Brianna, striking a pose and holding their hands in a "V" formation.

Brianna put her arm around Drishya and steered her towards the Year Six classroom.

"So, the second initiation is really simple," she

said. "But it's, like, totally the essence of what being in the Dream Squad is, like, all about."

"Totally," agreed Kimberley.

"So, like, let's role play," said Brianna, pointing at Elton. "What would you say to someone like him if he came up and tried to talk to you?"

"Er, I'd say hello?" said Drishya.

Brianna scoffed. "Wrong!" she said.

"Like, v v wrong," added Janet. "If someone like him comes up and talks to you, then you have to tell him that he's a tote-ser (**tot**al + lo**ser**)."

"Why?" said Drishya.

Brianna rolled her eyes. "Because it makes you look cool when you tell other people that they suck," she said.

"It's called a 'burn'," added Janet.

Drishya looked at Elton. She didn't want to burn him. Drishya didn't want to burn anyone.

"Okay," said Brianna, "you try. Burn me."

This was getting out of hand and Drishya had to stop it right now.

"Look," she said, "I'm really sorry but I don't want to join the Dream Squad. It's just not for me."

Brianna pursed her lips together. "Well, it's okay as a start," she said. "But you need to be, like, way more direct."

Kimberley nodded. "You gotta get mean, girl," she said.

Drishya pulled her sleeve down over her hand and put her thumb through the hole. "Okay," she said. "I think it's kind of sad that you are so down on everyone."

"Ooooooh, good one," said Brianna.

"I thought I wanted to join because when Hattie left I didn't have a best friend and I felt a bit lonely," continued Drishya. "I thought we might have stuff in common, but now I know we don't. I don't want to make fun of people to make myself look cool. I mean, that seems like a huge waste of time and maybe says more about how miserable you are than anything else."

Brianna stared at Drishya, then looked at Kimberley and Janet and all three girls began clapping.

"That was incredible," said Brianna. "You like totally crushed it. Great psyche analysis. That hit, like, really, really hard. You are totally in."

"Er, sorry?" said Drishya.

"Welcome to the Dream Squad," continued Brianna. "Anyone with burns that sick has to be in the gang."

"Like, totally," said Janet.

But before Drishya could say anything else, Ms Husk swept into the classroom.

"Right, everyone, sit down, please," she said.

Drishya looked around and saw Elton and Commodore grinning at her and giving her the thumbs up. Drishya smiled and gave the thumbs up back. At least one of her gangs was one she wanted to be in.

A CRIME AGAINST VEG

The second that the lunch bell buzzed, Drishya grabbed her bag and dashed out of the class. She heard Brianna calling her name but she didn't look back. She just ran until she reached the school hall, which was completely empty. Drishya heard raised voices coming from the kitchen. She walked past the V-850 vending machine, and over to the serving hatch. There was a strong smell of something horrible, like dirty socks or dog guffs, or dirty socks dipped in dog guffs, that hung in the air. Drishya held her nose and peeped through the hatch. She could see Mrs Clutch and her assistant, Mr Thicket, standing next to a large pot, looking angrily at Mrs Tittering. Their faces were red and sweaty and Mrs Clutch was jabbing her finger back out into the lunch hall.

"That thing, out there," she said, "is ruining our lunches."

Mrs Tittering held up her hands, trying to calm the situation. "It's just a vending machine, Val," she said. "It's not doing any harm."

"Not doing any harm?" shouted Mrs Clutch, her face going so red that Drishya wondered if she was in danger of exploding. "Not doing any harm? It's a monster. It's turning the kids into animals. Goodness knows what's in those scummy snacks it keeps pumping out."

"SkumSnax," corrected Mrs Tittering.

Drishya turned around and looked at the V-850. A few people had come into the hall and a queue was already beginning to jostle around the machine.

"Whatever the flippin' heckhole they're called," said Mrs Clutch, dropping her large spoon into the pot. "I've got a mountain of boiled broccoli that I can't shift."

She pulled out the spoon, which now had

several pieces of limp, grey broccoli on it. The broccoli had been boiling away for hours and so by now was more mush than veg. Being a strict vegetarian, such a crime-against-vegetables made Drishya's stomach turn.

"I have assurances from Mr Noel Skum himself that SkumSnax are made from one hundred per cent organic ingredients," said Mrs Tittering.

Mrs Clutch snorted.

"And besides," continued Mrs Tittering, "the machines have nearly all run out so I'm sure the children will soon be at that hatch wanting a delicious lunch from you."

Mrs Clutch scoffed and spotting Drishya waiting, hurried towards the serving area.

"CHOICE!" she yelled.

Drishya pointed at a pile of shrivelled jacket potatoes and watched as Mrs Clutch grabbed one and slammed it down onto her plate.

"CHOICE!" she yelled at Tom Boosbeck, who was next in line.

After picking up some cutlery, Drishya saw Elton and Commodore sitting at a table opening up their packed lunches. She looked at her small, hard jacket potato and sighed.

"Starting from tomorrow, I'm going to bring in sandwiches," she said to herself, and walked over to join them.

Drishya put down her lunch on the table. Commodore and Elton were staring at an open notebook.

"What's that?" asked Drishya.

"My tactical strategies and battle plans," said Elton. "I've taken a lot of inspiration from classic chess moves and openings. What do you think?"

Elton pushed the notebook across the table so that Drishya had a better view. She stared at the page. He had drawn tiny battle bots inside the Arena of Annihilation, then used coloured arrows to show the battle strategies.

"These are brilliant," she said, as an enormous noise exploded from the vending machine queue.

Drishya turned and saw Eddie Splott yelling something about there being "no more SkumSnax" at the top of his voice. She didn't know it but Noel Skum's super-concentrated flavour-powder was doing its devious addictive work. Drishya shook her head and turned back to Elton and Commodore.

"So, I've made a few modifications to G.E.O.F.F.," she said, reaching into her bag and pulling out her battle bot notebook. "If we're going to use the SKUM9 chip then the extra power means we can go for a much bigger spike on the back, and a piston flipper at the front."

"Rad," said Commodore, admiringly.

Drishya allowed a tiny smile to flicker over her

lips. "And I've covered G.E.O.F.F. with electrodes," she said. "They'll cover the whole bot in mini lightning bolts."

"Hmmm, a most excellent idea," said Elton. "If another bot starts beating G.E.O.F.F. up..."

"Then we give them a blast with the mini lightning, which will totally fry their circuits," said Drishya. "It will completely disable any predator."

"That could prove to be a highly effective strategy," said Elton.

"Triple Threat!" said Commodore, doing the Triple Threat sign of holding the three middle fingers of his right hand up and wiping them in front of his eyes. "We're going to win ROBOCALYPSE, for sure."

There was another roar of noise and Drishya

turned and saw the jostling queue of unhappy
vending machine customers charge at the V-850.
However, the vending machine was so heavy
that they all bounced off it.

"Machine empty," said the V-850, in its calm,
monotone voice before a metal shutter descended
that said, "SORRY I AM CLOSED".

THE THREE LAWS OF VENDING MACHINES

In an office, high up on the twenty-seventh floor of the tallest building in Dreary Inkling, Noel Skum stood in front of a huge map of the world. He stuck a red pin into it and stepped back to admire the hundreds and hundreds of other red pins that covered the map. A sign above the map read

GLOBAL DOMINATION
SKUMSNAX SALES LOCATIONS

"At this rate, I'm going to be a bazillionaire before the end of the year," he said to himself. "Maybe even a kajillionaire."

The phone on his desk began to ring. He looked at the caller display and saw that the call was coming from Dreary Inkling Primary School. He put on his hands-free headset and pushed the green "talk" button on the phone.

"Hello?" he said.

"Mr Skum? Mr Skum? Is that you?" shouted Mrs Tittering over the din of what sounded like a riot.

"Hello, yes, this is Noel Skum," said Noel Skum. "What can I do for you?"

He picked at his teeth with his pinkie finger. He knew exactly what she wanted. His sour, dismal mouth fractured into a smile.

"We need more SkumSnax, Mr Skum," said Mrs Tittering. "I'm afraid we've run out already and the children..."

She paused for a moment and Noel Skum heard the sound of shattering glass.

"...The children are very keen that we get some more as soon as possible."

Noel Skum pulled a piece of old food out of his

teeth, examined it and ate it again. "Well, as luck would have it," he said, "I have a new shipment ready for you. I'll bring it over personally, this evening." He paused. "Although, you will have to pay for this one."

There was the sound of muted screaming down the phone line.

"Yes, yes. Anything, anything. Oh, thank you, Mr Skum, thank you so much," said Mrs Tittering. "Now, I'm very sorry but I really must go. I think the staff room might have just caught fire."

Noel Skum's beady eyes twinkled with delight as the line went dead. "Well," he said. "How wonderful."

He took off his headset and threw it onto his desk. His intercom buzzed and a voice crackled through.

"Your one-thirty appointment is ready, Mr

Skum. Mr Remnant is here."

"Show him in," he said, walking back over to his map.

A moment later, a stressed looking Alan rushed in.

"What do you want?" snapped Noel Skum.

Alan had a terrified look in his eye. "It's gone crazy," he said. "The whole thing has gone flippin' crazy. We're getting orders in from schools and swimming baths and shopping centres all over the country."

Noel Skum smiled and walked over to the large window that looked out across Dreary Inkling. "It is exactly as I predicted," he said. "The super-concentrated flavour-powder makes my new SkumSnax irresistible to kids. Have you arranged to send out new supplies to my lovely vending machines?"

Alan nodded. "Yes, Mr Skum," he said. "But that's not all. There's a problem."

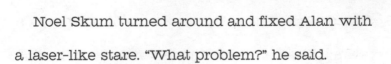

Noel Skum turned around and fixed Alan with a laser-like stare. "What problem?" he said.

Alan pulled a hankie out of his pocket and began mopping his sweaty brow. "Er, well, sir, it's the three laws of vending machines, the ones that we code into every single unit."

He pointed at a large sign on the wall, just next to the map.

THE THREE LAWS OF VENDING MACHINES

1. A vending machine must always provide delicious snacks to humans.

2. A vending machine must never hurt a human.

3. A vending machine must try and protect itself, unless it conflicts with other Vending Machine laws.

Noel Skum turned back to Alan and scoffed. "Yes, yes, yes," he said. "They're the laws that stop vending machines from going out of control and killing humans and taking over the world. What of them?"

"Well, Mr Skum," said Alan, squeezing his sopping-wet hankie out over Noel Skum's waste-paper basket. "It appears that our, er, I mean your vending machines were only programmed with the first law. We completely missed the other two."

Noel Skum walked over to his desk and sat down. "Are they dangerous?" he said.

"Oh no, not at all," said Alan. "No, no, no, no, no, no, no, maybe." Alan smiled nervously. "It's really very unlikely," he continued. "There would need to be a series of extraordinary and highly unusual coincidences. I mean, you'd need some sort of enormous energy surge to go through their circuits and even then, the machines would only turn rogue if there was something inside them that the energy surge could react with. The chances of anything bad happening are a million-to-one, at least."

Noel Skum smiled and stood up from his desk. "Good, so it's all systems go," he said, clasping his hands behind his back and pacing around his office. "Get on to the supply team. I want all those vending machines restocked by tomorrow. I will personally be seeing to Dreary Inkling Primary School myself."

"Yes, Mr Skum," said Alan, making feverish notes in his phone whilst Noel Skum continued to walk and talk.

"There are to be no mistakes," he said, smiling to himself. "Those machines are about to make me even more stinking, dirty rich and nothing is going to stand in my way." He bumped into Alan. "You're in my way," he snapped.

"Oh," said Alan. "Sorry."

A SERIES OF EXTRAORDINARY AND HIGHLY UNUSUAL COINCIDENCES

Drishya smiled as she walked home past the library on Wildhack Lane. She glanced up at the sign, which should have read,

THE DREARY INKLING PUBLIC LIBRARY

but because so many of the letters had fallen off, it now read,

HE REA   L   PUBLIC LI   AR

On their way out of class after last lesson, Triple Threat had hatched a plan. Drishya was going to finish the bodywork on G.E.O.F.F. that night and bring it into school tomorrow. Elton was going to bring in the SKUM9 microchip so that Drishya could fit the chip and Commodore was going to bring in his broken remote-controlled car. That way, they could finish G.E.O.F.F.'s circuits, mount it onto its wheels and properly test out how well it moved. But as Drishya daydreamed about winning **ROBOCALYPSE**, she turned the corner onto the high street and stopped dead in her tracks. The Dream Squad were sitting on a bench next to Mad Donner's takeaway. Brianna spotted Drishya immediately.

"Hey, Drishya," she called. "Over here."

Drishya trudged over. "Oh, er, hi," she said.

Janet looked at her and cocked her head to one side in a move that Drishya thought made her look very much like a constipated chicken.

"We were just practising," she said.

"Practising what?" said Drishya, more out of politeness than actual interest.

Kimberley looked at Janet who looked at Brianna and then all three stood up.

"This," said Kimberley.

She clicked her fingers and each member of the Dream Squad flexed their body into a different pose. Brianna stood with her hands on her hips, head

tilted to one side, her eyes
bulging like she was about to
be sick. Janet stood straight,
half-turned away from
Drishya, flicking her hair and

staring with such intensity she looked like she

had just farted in a shop and
didn't want anyone to know it
was her. Meanwhile, Kimberley
scissor-kicked her way around
the pavement,
one hand on
her hip, and

pouting her lips like they'd
been sucked into the tight
neck of an invisible bottle.

"We practise our poses so people know how ve-some we are," said Brianna.

"Now you're in the Dream Squad you've got to start pulling moves like this," said Janet. "And they take v v v v v v lots of practice."

"Mucho practice-o," agreed Kimberley.

Brianna linked arms with Drishya. "Come on," she said. "I've been thinking about some moves that you can start working on. Let's chalk (**ch**at + w**alk**)."

She began to steer Drishya down the street with Janet and Kimberley walking arm-in-arm behind them. Drishya took a deep breath. This had all gone far enough. She knew she had Peachy Keene's cardigan but the situation was getting ridiculous. Drishya didn't want to practise posing, she wanted to build things.

"Look," she said. "About joining the Dream Squad. I mean, it's not that I'm not grateful for the opportunity and everything. It's just that I really don't think—"

But before Drishya could finish what she was saying, the sound of beeping car horns drowned her out. She looked down the street and saw the hole that her mum had dug had grown in size. It was now so big that all the after-school traffic was stuck in a jam that stretched down the high street. The loudest honks were coming from a strange-looking car as it nudged its way past the roadworks. It looked to Drishya like it was hovering on a cushion of air.

HONK HONK HONK

Inside his hovercar, Noel Skum was going crazy. He was honking with one hand and applying glue to his wig with the other, all the while talking to Alan via his in-car videophone.

"Yeah, I just dropped off the supplies at Dreary Inkling School," he said, adjusting his hairpiece in the mirror. "The head teacher couldn't believe how much they were going to cost but she didn't want another riot from the pupils so she paid up, like I knew she would."

Noel Skum frowned and honked the horn again. "HURRY UP!" he yelled. "I'M A VERY BUSY MAN AND MUST NOT BE KEPT WAITING!"

He picked up a half-drunk can of orange soda and took a small swig. Just as he drove past the big hole in the road where the electrical work was taking place, Noel Skum threw the can out of his open window. The can bounced off a safety bollard and hit a large circuit board that Drishya's mum had been working on for most of the day, covering it with sticky orange soda.

"What?" she said, looking around for who had thrown the can.

The circuit board suddenly began sparking, and a huge surge of electricity rushed through its wires and out into the electrical system. The electrical system that supplied all of Dreary Inkling's power. The effects were instant and catastrophic. Bolts of electricity sparked along the overhead cables. One by one, all the street lamps glowed ten times brighter than usual before exploding and showering the length of the high street with shards of broken glass. Drishya's mum sat watching, bedraggled and bewildered, in a heap on the floor, her singed hair sticking up, and her face smudged with streaks of carbon.

And down the road at Dreary Inkling Primary School, a few moments after the school caretaker, Mr Dulé, had locked up for the night, the enormous burst of electricity surged through the vending machines. The V-850s shuddered and jolted as sparks flew out of them. After a few moments, once the sparking had finished, a quiet darkness descended throughout the school. The vending machines' control panels went blank, then they began to reboot, using their backup batteries. As they whirred and clicked back into life there was something different about them. The V-850s' green eyes blinked and turned red.

"System error," said the vending machine that was sitting just outside the staff room.

Its red eyes scowled in the dim light for a few seconds before they blinked again and turned back to green.

WEDNESDAY

AN EARLY MORNING BIN-JUICE SHOWER

The school was empty when Mr Jagger approached the vending machine outside the staff room, wearing only a shirt, a tie and a pair of pants. He had arrived early to school, as usual, dressed in his favourite cream suit. Unfortunately though, his inability to multi-task had made him spill hot chocolate all over his suit whilst trying to do some marking and a very tricky yoga move at the same time. So, here he was, standing in his

pants, in front of a vending
machine while he waited for
the wet patch on the front of
his trousers to dry.

He perused his
options and moved
over to the vending
machine's control
panel. As he did, the

V-850's eyes blinked and the red laser beam
flashed out and began scanning his face.

"Hello, Mr Jagger, what would you like?" it said
in its calm, monotone voice.

"Er, chocolatey beef SkumSnax, please," said
Mr Jagger. "I want to see what all the fuss is about."

The V-850 blinked and, with a whooshing

sound, delivered a packet of chocolatey beef SkumSnax. As Mr Jagger took the packet, he noticed something behind the vending machine's glass. It was something white and fluffy.

"Looks like Mrs Tittering's eye mask," he said. "I wonder what that's doing in there?"

"Chocolatey beef is the most popular of all the SkumSnax flavours," said the V-850 in its calm, monotone voice, interrupting Mr Jagger's train of thought. "In the last two days, over three hundred and fifty packets have been consumed in this school."

Mr Jagger forgot all about the eye mask and opened the packet. "Three hundred and fifty?" he said. "These things must be delicious."

Holding the bag up to his face, he took a sniff.

His nose immediately wrinkled. "Funny smell," he said. "A bit, er, er, binny."

Slowly, Mr Jagger pulled out one of the circular, crisp-like snacks and placed it delicately on his tongue. Almost immediately he wished he hadn't, as the SkumSnax melted, delivering its binny taste all around his mouth. Mr Jagger spat it straight out. The SkumSnax hit the side of the vending machine and slithered down onto the floor, leaving a trail of spittle in its wake.

"Uuurggggghhhhh!" he yelled, shoving the rest of the packet down the vending machine's recycling chute. "That was absolutely disgusting."

The vending machine whirred for a moment. "What did you say?" it said in its calm, monotone voice.

Mr Jagger stopped wiping his tongue and looked nervously at the machine. "Er, I, er, said that the SkumSnax tasted horrible," he said.

The vending machine whirred again for a moment and, suddenly, its eyes turned from green to red. "Oh dear me," it said. "I do hate an unhappy customer. Here, let me give you a refund."

A moment later, a jet of bin juice shot out of the recycling chute, completely soaking Mr Jagger. It went all over his hair and face and in his eyes and ears and up his nose, and all over his shirt and tie.

"WHAT'S GOING ON?" he managed to yell, before the robotic arms of the V-850 shoved a packet of chocolatey beef SkumSnax in his mouth, muffling his screams.

Mr Jagger staggered back away from the machine, slipping in a bin-juice puddle and falling in a heap on the floor. He looked up and saw the V-850 trundling towards him.

"Mmggffhfhfffmmm," he shrieked, through a mouthful of SkumSnax, as the vending machine's robotic arms grabbed his legs and began pulling him towards it. "Mmggffhfhffmm!"

The V-850 dragged poor Mr Jagger across the corridor floor and towards its waiting, gaping dispensing slot that looked like a gigantic mouth, yawning open. Mr Jagger struggled and struggled but the arms were too strong. First, the vending machine's dispensing slot swallowed Mr Jagger's legs, then his whole body, before finally, it sucked up his head as well. In a matter of seconds, Mr Jagger had been consumed by the vending machine and lay, dazed and covered in stinking bin juice, inside it, on top of some chocolatey beef SkumSnax, wearing only his pants and shirt and tie. The glass front of the machine was so thick that his sobs and cries for help were silenced. Then, with a clatter and crash, the metal shutter that said

fell down over the glass front so no one could see him either. Mr Jagger was completely trapped inside the machine.

Ten minutes later, Mrs Tittering wandered past the V-850 that was just outside the staff room and noticed that the metal shutter was down.

"That's funny," she said. "Mr Skum came and filled up all the machines last night. They can't have sold out already, school hasn't even started yet."

She turned and went back to her office, muttering to herself about how much money the machines were costing and that she was going to phone Noel Skum and give him a piece of her mind. As she closed the door of her office behind her, one of Mr Jagger's shoes was spat out of the vending machine with a kind of metallic burping sound.

"Pardon me," said the vending machine in its calm, monotone voice.

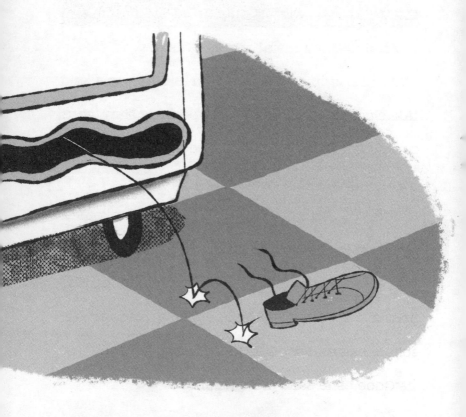

THE ATTACK OF THE SNACKS

"All clear," said Commodore, peeking through a curtain of coats. "Everyone's way too busy getting SkumSnax to bother us in here."

Drishya looked up from the makeshift workbench that Triple Threat had set up behind the rack of coats in the Year Six cloakroom. She had draped Peachy Keene's cardigan over her school bag and sat G.E.O.F.F. on top of that.

"Good," she said. "Let's begin."

Elton opened his rucksack and pulled out a plastic box. He opened the box and took out a plastic bag. Elton nodded at Commodore, then placed the bag on his outstretched palms. Elton reached inside the bag and pulled out a bundle of bubble wrap, which he carefully unravelled. Inside was an old grey sock. Very, very carefully, Elton put his hand in the sock and pulled out something small and grey with gold legs.

"You will be careful with it, won't you?" he said, handing the SKUM9 microchip over to Drishya.

"Of course." She nodded.

Drishya took a deep, calming breath. She knew she needed a steady hand to slot the SKUM9 microchip onto G.E.O.F.F.'s circuit board.

"Please don't damage the microchip," said

Elton, rather unhelpfully tapping Drishya on the shoulder at an incredibly crucial time. "My dad will kill me if it gets broken."

Drishya looked up at him and stared. "Stop panicking," she snapped.

Elton went quiet and Drishya returned to her work. One second later she felt a tapping on her shoulder again.

"What!" she cried.

"I just wanted to apologize, you know, for tapping you on the shoulder," said Elton in a very quiet voice.

Drishya slowly lowered the SKUM9 into place until she heard a satisfying click.

"Done," she said, breathing out a long, relieved sigh.

Drishya took four batteries and put them into G.E.O.F.F.'s battery pack.

"Okay, here we go," she said, looking nervously at Elton and Commodore. "Let's power it up."

Drishya's finger hovered over the "on" button for the briefest of seconds before she pushed it and held her breath. For a moment, absolutely nothing happened but then, one by one, three green lights lit up on G.E.O.F.F.'s domed orange back.

"It's alive," said Drishya, the excitement rising in her voice. "ALIVE!"

Elton and Commodore made the three-fingered Triple Threat sign and did a happy dance around the back of the cloakroom.

"Now we just need to give it some wheels," said

Drishya. "Did you bring the car in? I'll take it home tonight and weld it into place."

Commodore nodded and was just getting the smashed-up remote-controlled car from his bag when they heard some loud shouting coming from somewhere outside. Drishya walked over to the cloakroom opening, and the three of them peered around the corner and down the corridor. The shouting was coming from Eddie Splott.

"But I haven't had my TURN," he yelled at Mrs Tittering, who was standing next to the V-850.

"Break-time is over, Eddie," she said, as Eddie collapsed in a heap on the ground, sobbing.

Mrs Tittering rolled her eyes and looked at her watch. She wouldn't usually put up with this sort of nonsense but it had been a very stressful morning already. Mr Jagger hadn't turned up for work, she hadn't had her morning cup of tea yet, and Noel Skum was coming any minute to look at the vending machine outside the staff room.

"Oh very well," she sighed. "You can use the machine as long as you do it quickly and stop crying and you can only have one thing."

Eddie sniffed and dragged himself to his feet. "Thank you," he said, rubbing his nose on his sleeve. Eddie walked over to the V-850 and waited while it scanned his retinas.

The V-850's eyes blinked. "Good morning, Eddie Splott," it said in its usual calm, monotone voice. "How may I be of assistance today?"

"Er, chocolatey beef SkumSnax, please," said Eddie.

The V-850's eyes blinked twice. "I'm afraid chocolatey beef has sold out," it said. "Perhaps you would like another flavour?"

Eddie Splott stuck out his bottom lip and stamped his foot on the floor. "But I haven't tried any other flavour so they're probably horrible," he said, not noticing that the vending machine's eyes turned from green to red when he insulted the SkumSnax. "I want chocolatey beef."

The vending machine made a loud whirring noise. "It's alright," it said. "Why don't you try a packet of another flavour, for free?"

Suddenly, a packet of cheese and pickled egg SkumSnax fired straight out of the dispensing drawer and hit Eddie in the stomach.

"OW!" he yelled.

"All SkumSnax are delicious," said the vending machine. "Do not say anything bad about SkumSnax."

From the other side of the corridor, Drishya was watching everything.

"That's so weird," she muttered. "It's like it takes any negative comments personally."

POW POW POW POW POW POW POW

Before anyone knew what was happening, the V-850 fired out packet after packet in rapid succession.

"HELP!" screamed Eddie, as he took hit after hit after hit.

"Eddie!" yelled Mrs Tittering, trying to pull him out of the line of fire. But the V-850 just fired more SkumSnax.

POW POW POW POW POW POW POW
POW POW POW POW POW POW POW

By this time, teachers and pupils had started to emerge from their classrooms to see what all the commotion was. They watched in horror as Eddie and Mrs Tittering collapsed into a heap on the floor.

"We've got to do something," said Drishya.

"What?" said Commodore.

"I don't know," she said. "I'm thinking."

Still firing, the vending machine began to slowly turn away from Eddie and Mrs Tittering and began to attack other kids and teachers. The corridor was suddenly filled with the sound of screaming.

"You need to hurry up," said Elton, dodging three packets of banana and prawn SkumSnax that slammed into the wall behind him.

"Make it stop," wailed Betty Gabalfa. "Please, make it stop."

Drishya looked on as the vending machine fired off its barrage of flavour sensation in all directions. She noticed the extra-long flex on the back of the machine unwinding as it wheeled around the corridor.

"Of course," she whispered to herself. "It's so blindingly obvious."

Seeing her chance, Drishya began edging away from the others and over to the wall that the vending machine had been stationed at. As she did, the vending machine stopped firing

SkumSnax and turned to face the opening of the Year Six cloakroom, right where Elton and Commodore were still standing.

Elton grabbed hold of Commodore and hugged him close. "What are we going to do?" he yelled. "WHAT ARE WE GOING TO DO?"

The V-850 began moving towards Commodore and Elton and, as it did, started firing jets of bin juice out of its recycling chute, covering the corridor in a horrendous shower of stinking awfulness. Elton tried to run but the floor was so drenched that he slipped over. As he fell he grabbed onto Commodore and pulled him over too. The pair slithered helplessly on the floor as the V-850 slowly moved closer, its robotic wheels crushing anything that lay in its path, until...

The vending machine stopped, its display went dark and the firing ceased.

Commodore, Elton and all the teachers and pupils turned and looked at Drishya, who was holding the plug in her hand after yanking it out of the wall socket.

"You did it," said Elton. "You stopped the killer vending machine."

But the words had barely passed his lips when a loud whirring sound started coming from the V-850.

"Oh no," said Drishya, a look of horror flashing across her face. "It's on battery back-up. It's coming back to life."

SOMETHING VERY VERY BAD

An eerie low hum rumbled in the belly of the vending machine. Everyone watched and waited in nervous silence while it rebooted. Elton and Commodore edged over to where Drishya was standing.

"What's going to happen?" whispered Elton.

Drishya shrugged. "I don't know exactly but it'll probably be one of two possibilities," she said. "Either the system reboot will restore the vending machine's settings, essentially returning it back to normal. Or..." Drishya paused. "Its coding has been permanently damaged, turning it into an evil vending machine, capable of destroying the world."

Elton and Commodore looked at each other as the lights on the vending machine began flashing. Suddenly, the "future of lunch" jingle started playing and the V-850's eyes appeared on the display panel and blinked twice. They were green.

"Skum Industries 2000 V-850 series vending machine reboot complete," it said in its calm monotone voice. "All systems normal. Syncing with other machines in the area."

Ms Husk, Mr Flange and some other teachers rushed over to the enormous pile of SkumSnax on the floor and began to dig out Eddie and Mrs Tittering.

"Is it over?" said Mrs Tittering, a little dazed from her ordeal.

Ms Husk nodded. "I think it's going to be okay," she said. "I think it's all going to be okay."

A huge cheer from everyone in the school was cut short by shouting coming from down the corridor.

"WHAT ON EARTH ARE YOU DOING TO MY MACHINE?"

Everyone turned to see Noel Skum striding towards Drishya, who was still holding the vending machine's plug. Behind him, a bit further down the corridor, Alan Remnant tried to keep up.

"I-it went all weird and started firing SkumSnax at people," stammered Drishya, who was finding it both strange and horrible to be shouted at by her hero.

Mrs Tittering scrambled to her feet, brushing a packet of cheese and pickled egg SkumSnax off her shoulder.

"A very serious incident has been averted by Drishya's quick thinking," she said. "You owe us an explanation. Your machines are faulty and this one could have killed someone."

Noel Skum pulled a face like he had just smelled something really awful, like the current experimental cauliflower and fish head flavoured SkumSnax.

"FAULTY?" he yelled. "IMPOSSIBLE! MY MACHINES AREN'T FAULTY. THEY'RE TOO ADVANCED TO BE FAULTY. YOU'VE PROBABLY BROKEN THEM."

Mrs Tittering looked aghast. "We have most

certainly not broken them," she said.

Alan Remnant tapped Noel Skum on the shoulder. "Er, this does make sense given the alarming possibility discovered by our technical staff this morning," he said, pulling out a sheet of paper from his top pocket.

Noel Skum's eyes widened. "What alarming possibility?" he said.

"Yes, what alarming possibility?" said Mrs Tittering.

"Er, well," said Alan, trying to whisper. "The technical staff discovered that the chemical nature of bin juice can change if heated to a high temperature very suddenly. The bin juice can become volatile and react very badly with highly sophisticated circuitry."

"Meaning?" said Noel Skum.

"Well, in short," said Alan, "if the electrical surge reacted with the bin juice in the V-850s and corrupted their circuits, then because we forgot to programme them with all three Laws of Vending Machines, it's possible that they have turned into killer vending machines."

"Bin juice?" said Mrs Tittering. "You're saying that bin juice reacted with the surge of electricity? What does bin juice have to do with your vending machines?"

Noel Skum looked around nervously.

"Oh, it's what SkumSnax are made from," said Alan, before Noel Skum had the chance to say anything.

"WHAT???" yelled Mrs Tittering.

yelled everyone else. "Oh my GOD!" yelled Drishya. Eddie Splott fainted at the thought of the dozens of packets of chocolatey beef flavoured bin juice that he'd eaten in the last forty-eight hours.

"L-look, it's one hundred per cent organic matter," said Noel Skum, edging back down the corridor. "I-it's perfectly harmless to humans."

Mrs Tittering was about to give Noel Skum an overdue piece of her mind but before she could say anything she was interrupted by a strange trundling noise coming from somewhere behind her. Drishya turned and saw the other two vending machines rattling down the corridor and heading straight for them. One had its metal shutter down.

"That's weird," said Noel Skum, turning to Alan. "What's going on?"

The vending machines came to a standstill and sat humming for a moment.

"V-850s fully operational and ready," said one of them.

Suddenly, the metal shutter on the other machine flipped up and there, blinking back at them, was a trouser-less Mr Jagger, lying awkwardly on a pile of SkumSnax, clutching Mrs Tittering's eye mask.

"Norman?" gasped Mrs Tittering. "Norman? What have they done to you?"

All at once, the vending machines' digital eyes blinked twice and changed from green to red.

"Oh no!" whispered Drishya. "This is bad. This is very, very bad."

"We are fully operational and ready," said the nearest vending machine, "to DESTROY! DESTROY! DESTROY!"

The V-850s' red eyes glowed brightly and suddenly laser beams shot out of them, burning through walls and doors. Everyone started screaming again.

Drishya glared at Noel Skum. "DO SOMETHING!"

she yelled. "YOU MUST BE ABLE TO DO SOMETHING."

But Noel Skum wasn't listening. Both he and Alan Remnant were scurrying back down the corridor as fast as they could.

Drishya turned and looked at the Dreary Inkling teachers and pupils who were all screaming and running for cover. She grabbed Elton and Commodore and dragged them back into the Year Six cloakroom. There was no one who could save them. They were going to have to face the killer vending machines all on their own.

G.E.O.F.F. VS THE MACHINES

Drishya ran to the back of the cloakroom with Elton and Commodore following close behind.

"What are you doing?" said Commodore, as Drishya grabbed G.E.O.F.F. from the makeshift workbench behind the curtain of coats.

"I've got a plan," said Drishya. "Get your car. We'll use G.E.O.F.F. to fry their circuits."

Commodore ran to his bag and grabbed his old, broken remote-controlled car. "But how?" he said.

"You need to weld the base to the bot."

Drishya pulled a roll of electrical tape out of her bag. "This'll do," she said. "It won't look very pretty but there isn't anything that this stuff can't hold."

Then, working with electrifying speed, she wound the tape around and around the bot and the car until they were fixed together, making sure the tape didn't block the electrodes on top. Drishya pushed the "on" button and the sleek, orange body of G.E.O.F.F. quivered and started humming. Each of the lightning conducting electrodes that were arranged on its back activated with a pale blue glow, and one by one the three power-up lights right on the top of the bot's domed body lit up in green. Without saying a word,

Drishya put G.E.O.F.F. on the floor.

"This is crazy," said Commodore.

"Yeah," agreed Elton. "We can't use the bot, you've only just finished building it. We haven't even tested it."

"You got a better idea?" she said.

Elton lowered his eyes and shook his head. "No," he whispered.

"Right then," said Drishya. "This'll have to be G.E.O.F.F.'s test. Just pray it doesn't fail. Triple Threat, ready?"

Commodore and Elton looked at each other and nodded. "Ready," they said together, doing the three-fingered Triple Threat sign.

They peered around the corner of the cloakroom opening just as Rory Bummlers and Tom Boosbeck ran past screaming, followed by a V-850 trundling along shooting banana and prawn SkumSnax at them.

Drishya, Commodore and Elton stepped out into the corridor to a scene of total devastation. There were holes in the walls and floors, and lights had been ripped off the ceiling and were hanging down by their wires. Through a cloud of red dust, Drishya could see friends and teachers running and screaming as the three V-850 vending machines chased after them, firing their laser eyes, spraying them with bin juice or pelting them with packets of SkumSnax.

Drishya put G.E.O.F.F. on the floor and looked

at Commodore. "You ready?" she said.

Commodore held up the remote control and nodded. "Okay," he said. "Let's do this."

He turned on the remote control and pushed the paddles straight up but the bot didn't move.

"Come on, come on," said Elton.

"I'm trying, dude," said Commodore. "Is it on?"

Drishya checked. The green power lights were lit. "It's on," she said.

Commodore pushed the paddle up again. G.E.O.F.F. shuddered and whined but still didn't move.

"Maybe the bot's too heavy for the car," said Elton, flapping his arms up and down. "MAYBE IT'S TOO HEAVY!"

Drishya dropped to her knees and flipped G.E.O.F.F. over. A piece of electrical tape had been wrapped around one of the wheels and was stopping it from turning. Drishya ripped it away and put G.E.O.F.F. back on the floor.

"Try it now," she yelled.

Commodore pushed the paddles once again and this time G.E.O.F.F. sped away.

"That thing is really fast," said Elton. "Look at him flippin' go."

Drishya thought about her Nani Ji as she watched G.E.O.F.F. skid around some rubble and zip down the corridor.

"Small is nimble, small is speedy," she said. "Those vending machines might be bigger and more powerful but we can easily out-manoeuvre them."

Commodore swerved G.E.O.F.F. around an upturned bin and raced it towards the vending machines who were targeting a group of Year One kids trapped inside the I.T. room.

They reminded Drishya of a pack of animals that she had seen on a nature programme, working together to bring down their quarry.

"You need to get it right next to the vending machines!" she yelled, trying to make herself heard. "I've set it so that if the bot touches something for three seconds, the lightning will be activated."

Commodore nodded, dodged G.E.O.F.F. around the mangled wreckage of the photocopier and moved it alongside one of the V-850s.

"It's touching!" yelled Elton.

Drishya held her breath and counted.

"One."

She prayed that G.E.O.F.F. wouldn't break down now.

"Two."

She could see the electrodes were beginning to glow pale blue.

"Three."

ZZZAAAAPPPPPP

Lightning flashed over the curved surface of G.E.O.F.F. and spread all the way up the body of the vending machine causing it to judder and jolt to a standstill. It shuddered for a few moments, then a panel popped open on its side and out fell a jumble of wires and cables. And right in the middle of the tangle was a bright orange microchip.

"Look," shouted Elton. "It's the SKUM10 microchip."

The vending machine let out a great mechanical groan as smoke started billowing out. Then, after a loud bang, it toppled backwards into the I.T. room, disappearing from view. A pool of bin juice slowly spread out from inside the doorway, like blood from a murdered body.

Elton and Commodore cheered.

"We got him!" yelled Commodore.

"THIS JUST IN!" yelled Elton. "THAT WAS AWESOME!"

But Drishya didn't cheer or dance. "This isn't over yet," she said, nervously. "Quick, get G.E.O.F.F. out of there and after the next vending machine."

Commodore clenched his teeth and pulled the

234

levers down to get G.E.O.F.F. moving again, but nothing happened.

"What's going on?" said Drishya, running over and grabbing her motionless battle bot from the floor. The whole of G.E.O.F.F.'s shell was charred.

"Is it okay?" said Elton, as he and Commodore rushed over.

Drishya cradled G.E.O.F.F. in her arms.

"It doesn't have any power," she said, trying to hold back tears. "The lightning must have overloaded its batteries."

Commodore ran a hand through his mop of red hair. "Can you fix it?" he said.

Drishya shook her head. "Even if I had all my tools with me it would take at least a couple of hours," she said. "And we don't have that sort of time."

The sound of screams came from down the corridor.

"But there are still two more vending machines," said Elton. "What are we going to do?"

Drishya carefully put G.E.O.F.F. down behind the upended photocopier. She peered through the dust and saw the two remaining vending machines had trapped her class behind the protective glass outside the front office. The sound of laser fire and screams of panic echoed around the wreckage of the school. She looked helplessly at the terrified faces of her classmates, not

knowing what she could do to help. But then, just when all hope seemed lost, Drishya smelled something. One of the worst and most disgusting smells in the world. But it was a smell that gave her an idea. She turned to Elton and Commodore.

"I've got a plan," she said. "I need you to find the Dream Squad."

"What?" said Elton. "Why them?"

"I'll tell you later," said Drishya. "Just find them and meet me back here as fast as you can."

"Where are you going?" asked Commodore as the three of them ran back towards the cloakroom.

"I'm going to get some lunch," shouted Drishya as she sprinted off in the direction of the school canteen.

A DISGUSTING PLAN

Two minutes later, Elton and Commodore stood outside the Year Six cloakroom with the Dream Squad, who they had found hiding in the art supply cupboard. They all watched as Drishya ran back towards them, holding two large plastic tubs. Screams of terror echoed down the corridor.

"Good, you're all here," she said. "We need to get to work."

"What do you need us for?" said Brianna.

"We can disable those machines if we can get close enough to them," said Drishya. "I need someone to distract them and lure them back here."

"What's that got to do with us?" said Janet.

Drishya looked at each member of the Dream Squad. "The vending machines went out of control when Eddie insulted them," she said. "Those things take burns really seriously."

"So?" said Kimberley.

"So," said Drishya. "Who throws down the best burns in the school?"

Brianna, Janet and Kimberley's eyes widened as they suddenly understood what Drishya was talking about.

"The Dream Squad," they said together.

"Exactly," said Drishya. "I want you to do what

you do best. I want you to go out there and hurl insults at those machines. The meanest, nastiest things you can think of. When you start insulting them, they'll want to kill you and so they'll follow you. Just get them back here, we'll do the rest."

Brianna looked at Janet and Kimberley and the three of them nodded their agreement.

Drishya took off her cardigan and handed it to Brianna. "For luck," she said.

Brianna gasped. "Is this...?"

Drishya nodded. "Yup, it's Peachy's."

Brianna slowly took it from Drishya and put it on. "Thanks," she said. "It's amazing."

Brianna smiled at Drishya and it wasn't a sarcastic smile or a smile that was designed to show someone how uncool they were. It was a proper, genuine smile of friendship.

"Dream Squad, ready?" said Brianna.

"Dream Squad, ready!" shouted Janet and Kimberley.

Drishya gave the three Dream Squad members a big hug. "Good luck," she said. "I know you can do it."

Brianna nodded and the three of them ran down the corridor towards the sound of screaming.

"What are we going to do?" said Elton, as they watched the Dream Squad disappear around the corner.

Drishya smiled and pulled off the lids of the tubs she was holding to reveal foul-smelling, lumpy green gloop.

"We're going to broccolerize them," she said.

BURNS SO SICK THEY COULD BE FELT ACROSS HISTORY

Drishya, Elton and Commodore ran down the corridor and peered around the corner.

The two remaining vending machines had started to use their robotic arms to smash the glass that Mrs Tittering and the rest of Year Six were hiding behind.

Kimberley was the first to walk out into the corridor. She adjusted her beret so it sat at a highly jaunty angle, put one hand on her hip, and scissor-kicked her legs like they had never been scissor-kicked before.

"Hey, vending machines," she shouted at the top of her voice. "Over here."

The vending machines stopped firing and both swivelled around to look at her. Kimberley looked towards the vending machine that had Mr Jagger inside, who was still sprawled over some SkumSnax.

"Knock knock," she said, in a loud clear voice.

"Who's there?" said the vending machine in its calm, monotone voice.

"I'm up," said Kimberley.

"I'm up, who?" said the vending machine.

Kimberley held her nose. "Uurgh, I thought you smelled bad," she laughed. "But if you say you're a poo, now I know why."

"Woah," said Drishya. "That was brutal."

The V-850s blinked but before they could react, Janet appeared from around the corner, flicking her hair and staring with ferocious intensity.

"Hey, vending machines," she said, "when I heard that you two were A.I., I didn't realize that stood for Actual Idiots."

Drishya stood with her mouth agape. This was a savage verbal attack.

The V-850s blinked again and swivelled back and forth not knowing who to look at. Suddenly, Briana leaped out into the corridor with her hands on her hips, head tilted to one side, her eyes bulging like she was about to be sick.

"Hey, vending machines, my toaster's a better

machine than you," she shouted. "And I don't have a toaster."

Drishya looked on at this incredible scene. It was a privilege to be witnessing some of the greatest burns in history.

The V-850s blinked again.

"The humans are mocking us," said one.

"Yes," said the other. "We must destroy them!"

Both vending machines moved towards where the Dream Squad were standing and began firing their lasers.

"Come on, girls," yelled Drishya. "This way, they're following you."

Brianna, Janet and Kimberley ran back around the corner towards Drishya, who guided them into the cloakroom.

"This just in," said Elton, shaking his head in admiration. "That was amazing. I've never seen anything like it."

Brianna blushed. "Like, thanks," she said.

Drishya handed Commodore and Elton a tub of thick broccoli gunk each. Then she peeped around the corner and back down the corridor. The V-850s were heading towards them.

"You two ready?" she said. "Remember, aim for the eyes."

Elton and Commodore nodded.

"Good luck," said Janet.

"Yeah, like, good luck," said Brianna, walking over to Elton and giving him a kiss on the cheek. "You're going to be ve-some."

Elton's face and whole body froze with shock.

"Elton!" Drishya snapped. "Focus! Get into position and deploy the gunk on my mark."

Elton nodded and smiled at Brianna before moving to the door.

"Three, two, one," said Drishya. "GO!"

At the same time, Elton and Commodore both jumped out of the cloakroom and into the corridor. In perfect synchronization, they threw great handfuls of gunk at the vending machines, splattering the V-850s directly on their eyes.

"Emergency! Emergency!" said the vending machines. "Surveillance facilities are down. Cannot see anything."

When she heard this, Drishya ran out of the cloakroom and, using Mrs Clutch's masher, jemmied off the side of each of the V-850s.

"Illegal panel removal," they cried in unison. "Illegal panel removal."

But Drishya wasn't listening. She had to act fast, the vending machines had deployed their robotic arms, which were flailing around, trying to grab at her. She ducked out of the reach of one machine's arm and ripped out its bright orange SKUM10 microchip. The V-850 immediately shut down.

Then she moved over to the other machine, dodging its grasping arm, and tore out its microchip too. As it shut down, the glass front popped open and a hot, trouser-less Mr Jagger fell out from on top of a pile of chocolatey beef SkumSnax. He tumbled onto the floor and sat for a moment looking absolutely stunned.

"I've got snacks in my pants," he said, then burst into tears.

A second later, Mrs Tittering raced around the corridor followed by the rest of the Year Six class.

"You did it, Drishya," she said, a huge smile plastered over her face. "You saved the school."

Drishya put her arms around Elton and Commodore, who put their arms around Brianna and Janet and Kimberley.

"No," she said. "We did it. We saved the school.

All of us friends, together."

FRIDAY

ROBOCALYPSE NOW!

Drishya sat on a sofa in the **ROBOCALYPSE** dressing room. Next to her sat Nani Ji wearing a T-shirt that said "I ♥ KILLING ROBOTS" on it and staring at her tablet computer.

"Kill! Kill! Kill!" she yelled at the screen.

The tablet made a bleeping noise, then a sad "end-of-game" noise.

Nani Ji sighed. "I'm stuck on level three of **TIME VACUUM**," she said. "I can't seem to kill the final

Death Giver. It always sucks my face off before I can head-shot it."

Drishya stared at her grandma. "You play **TIME VACUUM**?" she said.

Nani Ji nodded. "Oh yes," she said, softly. "Next time you play, look me up, my username is BATTLE BOTTOM NINJA JI."

Drishya chuckled. "But I thought you hated technology?" she said.

Nani Ji put down her tablet. "You know something, Drishya?" she said. "You were right, I was wrong. The world changes, it always has and it always will. Technology is a wonderful thing, a miracle."

"Apart from the vending machines," said Drishya.

Nani Ji waved her hands like she was wafting away a bad smell.

"Oh, there are things that go wrong, like the vending machines," she said. "But look at all the good things that technology does. I LOVE my new tablet. I can get in touch with our family back in Mumbai any time. And think about your Uncle Bikram's asthma. Fifty years ago, it would have killed him, but today he takes the inhaler wherever he goes, and there's no problem. That is technology too."

Drishya nodded and gave her grandma a big hug.

"Now," said Nani Ji, as she stood up from the sofa. "I am going to take my seat in the audience with the others. We are all so proud of you, Drishya. So get out there and kick some robot botty."

As she left the room, Elton and Commodore bustled in. They were both wearing homemade TRIPLE THREAT T-shirts, although whilst Elton's was neatly tucked into his jeans, Commodore's  was hanging out and completely creased.

Elton was holding a copy of the local paper in his hand. "Did you hear about Noel Skum?" he said.

Drishya shook her head. Since Wednesday, when his vending machines went on the rampage, no one had seen or heard a peep from Noel Skum. There had been rumours that he had gone into hiding and had plastic surgery to change the way he looked. Elton showed Drishya the front page. It said:

DUMB SKUM GETS MAP-TRAPPED

EXCLUSIVE: SKUM'S WIG REVEALS ALL

The paper said that after running away from Dreary Inkling School, Noel Skum had gone back to his office. Knowing that the authorities would want to question him about his murderous machines and underhand bin-juice practices, he started to get rid of any evidence that connected him to the vending machines. First, he smashed up his computer with a hammer before shredding drawers and drawers of documents. But as he tried to take his GLOBAL DOMINATION map off the wall, it fell on him. When he'd tried to stand up, he found that the heavy map had landed on his black cape attachment, completely pinning him on the floor. He survived for the next twenty-four hours by eating dead flies and woodlice that were on his office carpet. The police said that he had been discovered with five packets of SkumSnax in his pockets but had found them so disgusting that he'd eaten dead insects instead.

"Unbelievable," said Drishya, shaking her head in disbelief.

She put the paper down as someone knocked at the door and a woman wearing headphones and a clipboard came into the dressing room.

"It's time," she said. "Off you go."

Drishya, Commodore and Elton walked out of the dressing room and down a brightly lit corridor. Neon lights were flashing all around them and the walls of the corridor were covered in pieces of broken machinery and large holes that looked like they had been bashed out by a wrecking ball.

"I can't believe we're actually walking down

the Corridor of Carnage," said Drishya, trying to make herself heard over the loud guitar music and the muffled roar of an expectant crowd.

"I know," said Elton. "This just in. This is the greatest thing that has ever happened!"

The three of them stopped at the end of the corridor and waited by a huge wooden door that looked like it could have been the entrance to a medieval castle. The crowd noise was really loud now and Drishya could feel the vibrations and hear the sound of a thousand people all stamping their feet.

"WHO DARES STEP THROUGH THE DOORWAY OF DEVASTATION?" boomed a deep, mechanical voice coming from somewhere over their heads.

Drishya, Commodore and Elton all looked at each other, smiling excited, giddy smiles.

"TRIPLE THREAT!" they screamed in unison.

"VERY WELL, TRIPLE THREAT. PREPARE TO ENTER THE ARENA OF ANNIHILATION!"

The huge door slowly creaked open and the full force of the crowd noise hit Drishya for the first time. Triple Threat walked through the doorway and into the Arena of Annihilation in a bit of a daze. Drishya felt like her head was swimming as she tried to take everything in. A camera operator circled around her as she looked up at the crowd. She'd never seen so many people in one place before and everyone was looking at her and chanting their team name.

"TRIPLE THREAT! TRIPLE THREAT! TRIPLE THREAT!"

Commodore grabbed her by the arm and spun her around. "Look," he said. "There's the Dreary Inkling posse."

Sure enough, Drishya could see the Dream

Squad, Mrs Tittering, Ms Husk and Mr Jagger sitting together and waving at them. At least, Drishya thought it was Mr Jagger but as most of his head was covered in bandages it was quite tricky to tell. Drishya noticed Brianna blowing a kiss. She turned and looked at Elton, who caught the kiss and put it in an imaginary top pocket. Then he made a heart symbol with his hands and threw it to Brianna, who caught it and pretended to wash her face with it. Drishya laughed and nudged Commodore, who had also seen it and was shaking his head in disgust.

"Sickening," he said. "Utterly sickening."

Drishya, Elton and Commodore made their way to the podium at the side of the Arena of Annihilation where G.E.O.F.F. was sitting, ready for action.

"One final systems check," said Drishya, as she unscrewed G.E.O.F.F.'s battle-shell and peered inside. There, in the middle of the circuit board, was one of the SKUM10 microchips that Drishya had taken from the vending machines.

"It fits okay then?" said Commodore.

Drishya smiled and nodded. "Perfectly," she said. "G.E.O.F.F. is going to be super-powered."

"I dunno about this," said Elton. "Aren't you worried it might turn G.E.O.F.F. evil?"

Drishya screwed the shell back on and flipped the battle bot over. "Nah," said Drishya. "It's just a processor, isn't it? It was the bin juice and the electrical surge that turned the vending machines bad."

She pushed a button on the remote control and G.E.O.F.F. shuddered into life.

Commodore shook his head. "But this is exactly the sort of thing that happens in books and movies and stuff," he said. "Just when you think the big killer robots have been wiped out, a little bit of them lives on and the whole cycle of destruction continues."

The three operational lights on the top of G.E.O.F.F. blinked into life.

Elton stared at them and pointed a shaking finger. "G-g-guys," he said. "Didn't those lights used to be green?"

Commodore turned and looked and sure enough, the lights on G.E.O.F.F. were now red.

"They did," he said, his voice trembling. "They

did used to be green. It's the microchip, it's corrupted G.E.O.F.F.! G.E.O.F.F. is going to take over the world."

"Somebody save us!" screamed Elton.

Drishya looked at them and rolled her eyes. "I needed new bulbs," she said. "The bot's lights were damaged by the vending machine. I didn't have any green ones so I used red ones instead."

Elton and Commodore looked at G.E.O.F.F. and then at each other.

"Oh," said Elton.

"Er, right," said Commodore.

Drishya put G.E.O.F.F. on the floor.

"TRIPLE THREAT, ARE YOU READY?" boomed the voice.

"Well," said Drishya, looking at Elton and Commodore. "Ready?"

Elton and Commodore looked at her and smiled. "READY!" they shouted.

Drishya watched and waited for two trapdoors to open on the other side of the Arena of Annihilation. When they did, two large battle bots appeared through a cloud of smoke.

"They're massive," said Elton. "Much bigger than G.E.O.F.F."

He was right, they were much bigger. One had a large hammer strapped to its back, the other had a circular saw whizzing on its front. Drishya looked up to see Nani Ji giving her the thumbs up in the crowd.

"Being small does not mean you are weak,"

she said, smiling. "Small is nimble. Small is speedy."

"**ROBOCALYPSE** BEGIN!" boomed the voice.

"And if all else fails," said Drishya, as Commodore pushed forwards on the levers of the remote control and sent G.E.O.F.F. hurtling across the Arena of Annihilation, "we just hit them hard when they're not looking."

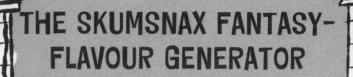

THE SKUMSNAX FANTASY-FLAVOUR GENERATOR

Congratulations. You are now the proud owner of your first SKUMSNAX FANTASY-FLAVOUR GENERATOR. It's exactly the same as the one that Noel Skum's flavour scientists use at Skum Industries HQ to invent all the amazing and delicious SkumSnax flavours, like cheese and pickled onion flavour, prawn and banana, and chocolatey beef flavour.

Using the SKUMSNAX FANTASY-FLAVOUR GENERATOR is simple. All you have to do is combine two flavours together.

FLAVOUR 1

The last piece of food you threw in the bin.

+

FLAVOUR 2

Something that's in your fridge right now.

= YOUR OWN SKUMSNAX FANTASY FLAVOUR

So using the SKUMSNAX FANTASY-FLAVOUR GENERATOR I've just created out-of-date yoghurt and broccoli flavoured SkumSnax. YUM! Happy flavour making.*

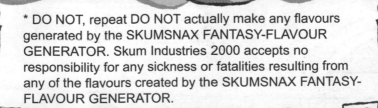

ACKNOWLEDGEMENTS

The hugest and most massive thanks to my editor at Usborne, Becky Walker, who is SO great that she would be in both Triple Threat AND the Dream Squad. Also, enormous thanks to everyone at Usborne for helping make this book the most colossialest killer book. Special mentions to Sarah S, Steph, Gareth, Will, Sarah C, Kat, and Mariesa.

Thanks to Liz Scott for being BRILLIANT and for all the taxi chats.

Mega thanks to my agent, Jenny Savill, at Andrew Nurnberg Associates for all her great advice and support.

Thank you to Elizabeth for being the original TRIPLE THREAT and to Joe and Sam for being brilliant joke-testers.

And thank you to all the vending machines who have dispensed delicious salt and vinegar corn snacks in my direction. I love you all. (Well, apart from the one at my local swimming baths that ALWAYS forgets to give change. And apart from the vending machine at the gym in Streatham that had those spiral dispenser arms that always got stuck so you had to get the manager to rescue your crisps and then the manager knew that you were eating crisps when you should have been working out. And also apart from the vending machine that used to be on the northbound platform of the Bakerloo line at Baker Street that would be a total stinkpants and take your money and not give you anything.)